HOT STONES • COLD DEATH
A MATTHEW ALEXANDER MYSTERY

Barbara Fleming

Silver Maple Publications • Yellow Springs Ohio

Copyright© 2001 by Barbara Fleming

All rights reserved

Hot Stones • Cold Death is a work of fiction, and all the characters, adventures or incidents depicted are purely imaginary. Any resemblance to actual persons, living or dead is entirely coincidental.

Printed in the United States of America
First Edition

The text of this book is
composed in Century Schoolbook

Cover Art Design by
Silver Maple Publications, Yellow Springs, Ohio

Cover Graphics by Brian Johnson for
Doran Design, Washington, D.C.

Book Design and Composition by
T. Schoch Enterprises, Yellow Springs, Ohio

Library of Congress Control Number 2001117024

Fleming, Barbara
Hot Stones • Cold Death / by Barbara Fleming

ISBN 0-9708970-0-6

Published by
Silver Maple Publications
Yellow Springs, Ohio

Dedicated, With Love to
My Mother, Mrs. Rosa Lee Durr,
My Husband
And My Daughters

HOT STONES • COLD DEATH

Primary Characters

DISTRICT OF COLUMBIA POLICE DEPARTMENT (DCPD)
ADMINISTRATIVE OFFICE
Jefferson Carter: Chief of Police

HOMICIDE DIVISION
Lloyd Cullison: Commander
Henry Bryant: Captain
Matthew Alexander (Matt): Detective Lieutenant
James Jackson (Jake): Detective Sergeant
Sam Johnson: Director, Forensics Laboratory

DISTRICT OF COLUMBIA MEDICAL EXAMINERS OFFICE
Stephen Mitchell, M.D.: Deputy Medical Examiner

SMITHSONIAN INSTITUTION
ADMINISTRATIVE OFFICE
Andrew Marshall, Ph.D. (Andy): Secretary
Colonel Wallace Kendricks (Wally): Director of Security

NATIONAL MUSEUM OF NATURAL HISTORY
William Fisher, Ph.D. (Bill): Director
Willis Brandt: Chief of Security
Earl Simms: Security Guard, First-shift
Joe Henderson: Security Guard, Third-shift
Lewis Smith: Security Guard, Third-shift
Henry Hughes, Ph.D.: Curator, Precious & Semiprecious Stones
Carlos Williams: Housekeeping Staff, Second-shift
Kofi Asante: Housekeeping Staff, Second-shift
Jimmy Wilson: Housekeeping Staff, Second-shift
Martha Darden: Assistant Curator, Native American Collection
George Bayless: Curator, Native American Collection

NATIONAL PARK SERVICE POLICE
Captain Ronald Dawkins: Superintendent of Parks for the District of Columbia

HOWARD UNIVERSITY
Anthony Phelps, Ph.D.: Professor of History & Anthropology

MATTHEW ALEXANDER'S FAMILY
Carla Alexander, Ph.D.: Wife & Clinical Psychologist
Robert Matthew Alexander: Two-Year-Old Son
Jennifer Elizabeth Alexander: Four-Year-Old Daughter

CHAPTER 1

Earl Simms watched from a distance as the crowd grew in front of the information desk. He shook his head in disgust at the rising chorus of complaints as Janice, the receptionist, dished out her usual mixture of misinformation and confusion. After observing the chaos for several minutes, he reluctantly left his security post at the mall entrance to the Museum of Natural History.

"What's the problem, Janice?"

"I can't find this Canadian tour group in the computer, Earl. He claims his company scheduled a guided tour for 10 o'clock this morning," Janice pouted while pointing an accusing finger at a frustrated, middle-aged tour director.

"Are any of the docents here, yet?" Earl asked.

"No, but they aren't supposed to begin guided tours until ten-thirty, anyway," Janice answered.

All the tour members sent up a howl of protest at the prospect of yet another delay.

"See here, Miss, it's just nine-thirty. You can't expect us to stand around in this lobby for another hour waiting for your staff to arrive. This is the worst service we've had since we've been in the States," the tour director loudly complained.

"It isn't my fault you're not in the computer," Janice complained just as loudly.

"It's nobody's fault, Janice. Even if they were in the computer, they still couldn't get a guided tour until ten-thirty," Earl insisted.

"That's right," Janice readily agreed.

"Why don't you let your group browse through the museum until ten-thirty. We ought to be able to work you in by then," Earl suggested.

The tour director threw Janice a dirty look before consulting with the group of elderly men and women, who slowly dispersed throughout the museum.

Thirty minutes later, Earl Simms was manning his station when he heard a series of high-pitched screams from the east wing of the museum. He quickly left his post and ran toward the screams. Just as he entered the *Cultures of Africa* exhibit, he collided with a half dozen elderly white women from the Canadian tour group, all howling hysterically.

When the women saw Earl, they stopped screaming and started pointing in the opposite direction. Only one of the women mounted the courage to go back into the exhibit with Earl. She took him over to the African village diorama and pointed toward two of the tribal figures at the back of the exhibit.

"Lord have mercy! What in God's name happened here?" Earl asked as he stepped into the exhibit to get a better look. He very cautiously wove his way through an elaborate African village diorama of half a dozen conical thatched huts and at least a dozen figures of men and women dressed in ritual costumes, including two figures on stilts, until he approached the very dead, grotesquely staged bodies of two young black men. One victim was limply sprawled across the stump of a tree, his upper body leaning awkwardly against the wall, his head savagely twisted toward his right shoulder. The other victim was propped against a tree trunk with both arms hanging over the limb supporting the weight of his corpse, his head thrown back at a bizarre angle as if the neck had been snapped in two.

Earl shivered as the dead man on the stump looked at him out of vacant eyes. It was clear from the bullet wounds to their bodies that both men had been shot to death and that they had bled profusely from the wounds. Earl grimaced at the smell from the release of the victims' sphincter and bladder muscles. He also noted that the animal-skin loin cloths they were wearing had been twisted to expose their genitals and that the victims' ritual costumes also included elaborate ostrich-feather headdresses and beaded collars. There was a thick layer of yellow grease smeared on both bodies.

The lone tour member fled the scene just as other museum staff and security guards ran in. Janice, the clerk from the information desk, was the last to arrive. She elbowed her hefty two hundred fifty pounds through the crowd in front of the exhibit to get a first-hand look, then promptly shrieked and fainted. It took two security guards and a staff person to break her fall and to maneuver her hefty bulk through the crowd and into the ladies room, where they placed her on a sofa and called for first aid.

The Chief of Museum Security, Willis Brandt, was grim when he arrived. He found Earl at the front of the African village diorama, as far away from the bodies as possible.

"The last thing we need right now is all you people milling around in here!" Chief Brandt shouted at the crowd before directing the security guards to chase nosy staffers back to their posts.

"The director hasn't arrived yet, so I called Colonel Kendricks," Brandt told Earl Simms. "Speak of the devil," he said as he turned to find the Smithsonian's Director of Security, Wallace Kendricks, striding purposefully in his direction.

"What the hell's going on, Brandt?"

"We have a double murder on our hands, sir."

Kendricks stopped in mid-stride as he absorbed the news.

"Tell me you're lying, Brandt."

"I wish I could, but the bodies are right over there. See for yourself."

Reluctant to leave the site of so much excitement, staff members ignored Chief Brandt's directive and gingerly stepped aside to make a path for Colonel Kendricks to the front of the murder scene. He simply stood and glared at the two bodies. Chief Brandt looked sheepishly toward his boss anticipating the worst, but Kendricks said nothing.

His silence was as ominous as the warning looks that passed among the security guards at the scene.

He finally spoke.

"Any idea when this happened, Brandt?"

"The first I knew about it was when Simms rang me about twenty minutes ago. I got up here as fast as I could. Simms got here sooner, but he doesn't know any more than I do."

"What happened in there, Simms?" Kendricks asked.

"Somebody killed those two men and left their bodies in the diorama, sir, with their privates exposed like that."

"That's obvious, Simms. You got any idea how long they've been dead?"

"When I went back there to look, I saw their blood was all congealed, with this yellow liquid floating around it; but I don't know how long they been dead."

"Are their bodies still warm?"

"Jesus, I didn't touch them, Colonel Kendricks."

"Give me a break, Simms," Kendricks said as he stepped inside the exhibit. "What the hell were you messing around in here for if you weren't going to find out how cold they are?" Kendricks walked over to the bodies and touched each dead man on the cheek. He also checked the pulse on the carotid artery, confirming what everyone else knew from just looking at the bodies . . . stone cold dead.

"Maybe they're Africans, sir," Earl hesitantly offered.

"And just what the hell is all that yellow grease smeared on them?" Kendricks asked as he violently wiped his hands on his handkerchief and catapulted the offending item into the trash bin.

"I don't know, sir" Earl replied.

"Even if they are Africans, Simms, they got no damned business dressed like that in one of our exhibits. Brandt, call the Park Police and then get the secretary's office for me. Tell them we have an emergency down here. Simms, clear these nosy-assed people the hell out of here right now, and cordon off this exhibit at both ends. I don't want anybody who isn't authorized coming through here. Jesus Christ! A double murder in the Museum of Natural History!"

"Do you want me to cover their privates, Kendricks?"

"Don't touch a damned thing, Simms. Leave them just like you found them."

Brandt finished his call to the Park police before ringing the secretary of the Smithsonian, Andrew Marshall. He gave the telephone to Kendricks.

"Wallace Kendricks here for the secretary. It's an emergency! . . . I said it's an emergency, so put me through to the secretary, now! This is Wallace Kendricks, sir. We've got a nasty problem in the Museum of Natural History. Two men have been killed over here . . . That's right, sir. They've been killed, shot to death. We found their bodies in a diorama in the *Cultures of Africa* exhibit. Actually, some tourists found them there this morning. All hell has broken loose over here. We don't know who killed them or how long they've been dead; but from the looks of things it happened late last night . . . We just found their bodies 30 minutes ago. I've put a call into the Park police for assistance, so they should be here any minute . . .I agree with you, sir. It's a very serious situation. I think our best bet is to contain it as tightly as possible . . . No, sir. Nobody on the day-shift admits seeing or hearing anything so far. That's why I think it must have happened late last night . . . I see your point, sir, but if we close the museum, that'll alert the press immediately; and if the media smell anything like murder they'll be all over us in no time flat . . . The museum has been open for almost three hours now, sir, and things look pretty normal considering what's happened . . . Well, yes, sir. I agree that two murders at the Smithsonian are very unusual. . . No, sir. I don't feel that the visitors are in danger. The bodies are stone cold, so they've been dead for several hours. I wouldn't keep the museum open if I thought so. I think the killer has put a lot of distance between him and the Museum of Natural History, a lot of distance . . . I think it might be better if you didn't come over here, sir. That way, the press won't be able to question you about the bodies. I'll keep you informed."

After Kendricks rang off he called the Director of the Museum of Natural History, William Fisher. His conversation with Fisher was brief.

"He's on his way down, Brandt. Of all the museums at the Smithsonian, why did it have to be Natural History? I can't do a damned thing right as far as Fisher's concerned. Why did it have to be Natural History?"

"Here he comes," Brandt said as Kendricks turned to find William Fisher charging toward them through the *Stone Age Mammals* exhibit, grey suit coat flying, nostrils flaring, chest heaving, face contorted with rage. Fisher rushed past

Kendricks and Brandt to the exhibit where he confirmed the murders for himself. He stared long and hard at the bodies before addressing Kendricks."

"This is your fault. If you knew what the hell you were doing, this would never have happened."

"You don't know what you're talking about, Fisher."

"The hell I don't. Where was your security when these men were being murdered? Where were your guards, Kendricks?"

"These men were killed last night. You know what the budget cuts did to third-shift security. I had to lay off 10 men, and three of them were from the third-shift."

"What was the point in installing that expensive computerized security system if you still need security guards all over the place? There are dozens of security cameras in the museum. If your staff weren't asleep on the job, this would never have happened."

"Don't you tell me anything about guards staying awake, Fisher. I've tried to fire that drunk, Joe Henderson, twice. I had him dead to rights last time till you stepped in and stopped me from getting rid of him. He was manning the security console last night, thanks to you."

"Joe Henderson has a bona fide disability."

"Since when is showing up for work pissy drunk every night a disability?"

"I think this conversation has gone far enough, Kendricks."

"It's Colonel Kendricks to you, Fisher."

"So, what the have you done about this situation so far, *Colonel* Kendricks?"

"I called the Park Police, and I called the secretary to tell him what's happened."

"What business is it of yours to call Secretary Marshall about what happens in my museum?"

"I'm director of security for all the museums. I'll call the secretary or anyone else I damned well please when two men are brutally murdered in one of our facilities."

"The Museum of Natural History is my responsibility, Kendricks. You know you should have informed me about the murders before you called the secretary."

"Considering the mess we're in, Fisher, quibbling over protocol is a waste of time. But you're free to call the secretary anytime you please."

"I don't need you to tell me that."

"Here come the Park police," Brandt volunteered as all three men turned to find Captain Ronald Dawkins and three of his men entering the exhibit from the Mall side of the museum.

Lean, wiry, asthmatic, and chronically red-faced, Captain Dawkins wheezed his way to the front of the crowd standing before the murder scene.

"Jesus, Wally, what a sight," Dawkins rasped as he shook hands with Colonel Kendricks and introduced himself to Bill Fisher.

"When were they killed?" Dawkins asked, speaking directly to Kendricks.

"To tell the truth, I don't know when they died, Ron. When I touched the bodies there they were cold and clammy; so I'm guessing it must have happened during third-shift when the museum is deserted. We just have two guards on duty during third-shift because of budget cuts. Besides that, somebody would have heard something if they had been shot this morning."

"You're probably right, Wally, but third-shift covers a lot of territory. What the hell are they dressed like that for? And what is that stuff smeared all over them?" Dawkins asked as he peered at the bodies across the top of the mouth inhalant he was using.

"You got me there, Ron."

"So let's see what we have here. Two black men dressed up like African warriors break into the Museum of Natural History after midnight where they die in an African village diorama? Kind of farfetched isn't it, Wally?" Dawkins asked.

"Bizarre is more like it," Kendricks replied as he moved away from prying ears and motioned for Dawkins and Fisher to follow him. "Look Ron, we've postponed calling the District Police because we wanted to get your take on this situation first. Once they get here, the shit's going to hit the fan. How do you size these killings up?"

"Your guess is as good as mine, Wally. I don't see a weapon over there," Dawkins stated as he looked toward the diorama.

"Earl Simms checked the diorama before we got here. He didn't find a weapon in there."

"You mean he's already walked through there?"

"Yeah, he walked through there before I got here. Earl wouldn't touch the bodies; and I had to know whether they were still warm. So I went in there, too."

"Jesus, Wally. What kind of crime scene are you running here? Make sure you don't let anybody else in there. There's evidence in that scene, and you don't want it contaminated or destroyed before the investigation starts."

"I'm glad somebody knows what they're doing," Fisher snidely remarked.

Kendricks ignored the jibe.

"Chief Brandt is trying to locate the names of everyone who was in the museum during third-shift last night; but the staff sign-in log is missing."

"What do you mean, it's missing, Kendricks?" Fisher demanded.

"Just what I said. The sign-in log for the third-shift is missing. That drunk, Joe Henderson, was on the security console last night, so it's a good bet he didn't enter the list into the computer. That's your boy, Fisher."

Bill Fisher gave Wallace Kendricks a look of pure hatred before returning to the murder scene. Kendricks and Dawkins walked out of the exhibit area into the second floor rotunda where they stood talking under the African Bush Elephant as visitors moved through the museum totally oblivious to the two murdered bodies in the diorama and to the potential danger that still lurked.

"What's with you and Fisher, Wally?"

"Don't get me started, Ron. So, what other steps can we take to shore this situation up?"

"There's not a whole lot I can recommend at this point, since I know so little about what the hell happened last night. But first thing I'd do if I were you is to get the third-shift guards back in here before the District Police get to them. You need to get their stories so you can reconstruct what went down."

"They've been gone for five hours. There's no way we can get them back here before we call the District Police in."

"It's better to go over to their houses than telephone them, Wally. They'll be more truthful if you're looking them in the face. Besides, there's no law against getting their versions of what happened before the police do. I'd rather know than be surprised."

"Yeah, I see what you mean. There's the third-shift security tapes, too. I'm sure the District Police will want to see those tapes first thing."

"They may not ask for the video tapes right away, if you don't mention you have them. That way, you'll have time to review the tapes for yourself."

"Christ Almighty. When will I have the time to watch tapes with the museum full of police?"

"The fun and games have just begun, Wally. This situation will get a whole lot worse before it gets better, believe me."

"How many men can you loan me, Ron?"

"I'll leave the men I brought with me for a couple of days, but that's the best I can do, buddy. We've laid off more staff than you have."

"Three is good. If I detail three of my guards, that ought to be enough."

"Once the press and the public get wind of what's happened, you'll wish you had a hundred men at each end. Don't let those Canadian tourists get away without talking to the women who found the bodies. What they saw could be important. I'd get on those tapes right away if I were you, Wally."

"Yeah, you're right," Kendricks replied as Brandt walked over to them with a worried look on his face.

"He didn't enter the sign-in list, Colonel Kendricks; and I still can't find the hard copy anywhere. The first-shift guard swears it wasn't there when he took over."

"No use crying over spilt milk, Brandt. I'll ask Joe Henderson about it when I see him later today. The only thing to do now is to get the security cordon in place. Absolutely no one goes into the exhibit without my permission, Brandt. Is that perfectly clear?"

"No problem, sir. I'll get on it right away," Brandt replied as he headed back to the murder scene.

"It looks like your Canadians are getting ready to leave, Wally," Dawkins said, pointing to the group of elderly white tourists lining up near the mall entrance to the rotunda.

"Damn, you're right. What time is it?"

"Twelve-thirty."

"You've got to keep them here until the District Police arrive, Ron."

"You know I don't have jurisdiction in a homicide case, Wally. How the hell am I supposed to keep them here?"

"They don't know that. Pull rank on them. Tell them they can't leave until the District Police talk to the ladies who found the bodies."

"Jeez, what'll you want next, my firstborn?"

Kendricks smiled as he placed a call to Fourth District Police Commander, Lloyd Cullison, a personal friend who had gone through basic training with him at Fort Benning, Georgia. As he was talking to Commander Cullison, Kendricks watched an irate bus driver and several of the more assertive tour group members get into a heated argument with Ron Dawkins. Dawkins stood his ground, but it was clear that he needed reinforcement. Before he rang off, Kendricks quickly explained the situation at the museum to Cullison and urged him to send his men down as quickly as possible.

"God! What a day this is going to be," Kendricks muttered to himself as he walked over to assist Ron Dawkins.

CHAPTER 2

When Lieutenant Matthew Alexander arrived for his meeting with Homicide Division Commander Lloyd Cullison at noon on Wednesday, he found the commander drinking a cup of freshly brewed coffee in his spacious office on the first floor of Fourth District Headquarters.

"What's up, Lloyd?"

"Help yourself to some coffee, Alexander. I got a call from Colonel Wallace Kendricks over at the Smithsonian. He's their director of security. Kendricks and I go way back to basic training at Fort Benning. He's a good friend, Alexander, so I want you to do everything you can to assist him."

"Assist him with what?"

"Double homicide. They've found two stiffs, black men shot to death inside the Museum of Natural History."

"Sounds like one of the curators freaked out big time. When did it happen?"

"Kendricks didn't give me many details when he phoned; but he thinks it happened late last night."

"You say the stiffs are two black men?"

"Yeah, that's what Kendricks said."

"Do they know who did it?"

"Don't have a clue. Looks like the shooter was a thorough son of a bitch."

"Was anything stolen?"

"Wally didn't say."

"Is there anything else I need to know?"

"I promised Wallace Kendricks we'd help him out, so try not to make his life miserable, Alexander. You know what a goddamned prick you can be."

"I'm immune to flattery, Lloyd," Matt replied as he rose to leave. "Thanks for the coffee."

"Oh yeah, Alexander. I forgot to tell you that Captain Bryant is already on his way to the Smithsonian."

"Whose case is it, Lloyd, mine or Bryant's?"

"It's your case, but I trust Bryant's judgment. He's steady and he never does an end run around the chain of command like some people I know. I want him on this case, Alexander."

"You want him, you got him," Matt icily replied before returning to his second floor office.

"What's up?" Jake asked.

"Double homicide at the Smithsonian. Lloyd's put his trusty bloodhound Bryant up to sniffing around my case again. Call forensics and tell Sam to meet us on the second floor of the Museum of Natural History, yesterday."

"How many District homicides does that make this year, man?" Jake asked.

"One hundred five and counting."

"And it's just the beginning of June. Man, the District ain't a fit place for a dog to live," Jake said as they headed for the parking lot. "D.C. used to be a real nice place, partner; but Lord knows, it ain't nothing but a shit-hole now."

"If it's a shit-hole, Congress and the President are in it up to their armpits, man."

"Tell me something I don't know already. If it wasn't for those assholes dragging their feet on cleaning up the drug trade we could get rid of crime in the District. That's what killed this city, partner, cocaine. We've been fighting drugs for years, but there ain't never been nothing like this here cocaine. I thought heroin was a trip, but it ain't shit compared to crack cocaine."

"Our so-called politicians talk about crime all day long and never mention drugs. It's like they're from outer space somewhere, Jake. How the hell can you fight crime in the District or any other major city if you can't stop the drug trade? Seventy-five percent of the murders in D.C. last year were drug-related."

"I'm sick and tired of it, Matt" Jake replied before he pulled into southbound traffic on Georgia Avenue. "I used to think what we did out here made a difference, but it don't matter a rat's ass anymore. Soon as you get started on one homicide, up pops the next one. We ain't doing nothing but chasing our tails, man, chasing our tails."

"If we don't do it, Jake, who will? You see the way white officers are hauling ass out of the District. We had more early retirements last year than over the previous five years combined. They don't think black folks are worth the risk anymore, man. If we don't try to stop the madness in our own community, who will?"

"We can't stop it as long as black neighborhoods are

saturated with drugs. It ain't about nothing but money for the drug kingpins, man. More money than the greedy assholes can ever spend, but what do they care as long as they add zeros to their net worth?" Jake complained as he continued south on Georgia Avenue toward the Mall.

"You're too young to remember how hard it used to be to make it, Matt, back in the 40's and 50's when everything was segregated and racist as hell. My mama and daddy sharecropped 30 acres of cotton for old man Tolliver in the Mississippi Delta for damned near 25 years. There were 10 of us children and everybody, including my sisters, worked like mules under that broiling hot Delta sun, bringing that cotton crop in; and every year that racist son of a bitch Tolliver would cheat my daddy out the money he made on his share. It broke my daddy's heart, man. He died when he was only 49 years old. That old white doctor said he died from congestive heart failure; but my daddy died of a broken heart from working so hard and having everything he worked for stolen by that cracker. We had to put in a huge garden every year just to feed ourselves, had to raise chickens and butcher hogs, too. When I look back, I don't see how we worked that hard; but back then, black people still had hope we could make a better life for ourselves. We still believed that if we got an education, and worked hard, and treated people right, and believed in God, everything would work out in the end."

"The only things young people believe in now are the almighty dollar, and a gun," Matt replied.

"Yeah, whatever happened to hope?" Jake asked as he made a right on Constitution and headed for the Museum of Natural History.

"It's hiding out with the rest of the American dream, Jake."

"Yeah, waiting for something or somebody to show us what it means to live like decent human beings again. This is a godless country, man. It's saturated with death and death dealing."

"Speaking of death, looks like there's no parking near the Museum of Natural History."

"You're right. I'll let you out here."

"Meet me on the second floor, Jake. Ask for Wallace Kendricks, if you can't find me."

When he reached the crime scene, Matt found three security guards manning the entrance to the crime scene. One of the guards escorted him inside the exhibit to Colonel Kendricks.

"This is where we found the bodies, lieutenant," Kendricks stated after giving Matt a rundown of what had transpired at the crime scene.

"Where are the Canadian women, now?"

"Captain Bryant talked to them before you got here. After he took their statements, he let their bus leave."

"Damn! How long have they been gone?"

"No more than 15 minutes."

"Which security guard did you say got to the scene first?"

"Earl Simms. I'll get him for you," Kendricks replied as Sam Johnson, the Homicide Division Forensics Specialist, and his two criminalists, Lois and Ruby, approached from the opposite end of the exhibit.

Sam stopped in front of the crime scene before walking over to Matt and unloading his equipment.

"What the hell happened, Alexander?"

"You tell me, Sam. Two stiffs dressed like tribal warriors, greased from head to toe, snuffed in an African village at the Museum of Natural History."

"This is some bizarre shit. What the hell does it mean?"

"Your guess is as good as mine."

"Who's the shooter?"

"Don't have a clue."

"What do you know, Alexander?"

"Not nearly as much as I'd like, Sam," Matt replied as he walked over to Captain Henry Bryant, his supervisor at the Homicide Division and a man Matt detested as the handpicked lackey of the Division Commander, Lloyd Cullison.

"Who's in charge of this homicide investigation, Bryant?"

"You are, Alexander, but you know the commander asked me to troubleshoot. You also know what prima donnas these Smithsonian people are."

"If I'm in charge, what business did you have letting that tour group leave?"

"I don't know what you're . . . oh yeah! The Canadian tourists. There were only five or six women on the bus who saw the bodies, Alexander. I took their statements," Bryant indicated as he passed a spiral notebook to Matt.

"They all saw the bodies at the same time; and the security guard says they all ran out of there screaming like their heads were on fire."

Matt leafed through the notebook and was disgusted by what he found. "You call these statements, Bryant?"

"The bus driver was raising holy hell about getting back to Toronto on time."

"I don't give a shit about that. You shouldn't have let those witnesses leave before I got here."

"I got the names, addresses, and telephone numbers of everybody who saw the bodies. I told you they didn't know anything else."

"And who's going to pay to send someone to God knows where in Canada, if we find out they do know something, Bryant?"

"I made a judgment call, Alexander; so live with it."

"Do me a favor, Bryant, and save your judgment calls for your own investigations," Matt insisted as Steve Mitchell, the District's Deputy Medical Examiner, walked over and joined them.

"What's the deal, Steve?" Matt asked.

"My guess is they've been dead 10 to 15 hours, give or take a couple. There's still some rigor, so it probably happened between one and three this morning. They were shot in the head first, in the temple, then they were shot through the heart. The killer knew exactly where to place the bullets. Not as much blood on the chest of the one who's sitting down. He was already dead when he took the shot through the heart. The one who's standing up bled more. He's the one who didn't die right away

33

from the head shot."

"Any evidence of the bodies being moved?"

"None that I can see. My guess is they were shot in the exhibit, but I could be wrong."

"Did the bullets exit the bodies?"

"Nope. Had to be a small caliber weapon. No exit wounds on either body."

"That makes our job a lot easier. What do you make of that grease on them?"

"Strange. Why are they dressed like that? Are they Africans?"

"So far, the staff claims they don't know jack shit about who they are or what happened, but I'm not buying that."

"Yeah, I know what you mean. Somebody's got to know something," Steve agreed as he watched Sam take pictures of the bodies and the crime scene.

Matt looked up from talking to Steve to see his partner, Jake, standing in front of the exhibit.

"Damn!" Jake volunteered, "This is some funky mess! How long they been dead?"

"I'll know more about the time of death when I finish my tests," Steve replied.

Brandt and Kendricks looked like men on a mission as they left the crime scene and moved swiftly through the museum to Brandt's first-floor office, where they began a frenzied search for the home addresses and telephone numbers of Joe Henderson and Lewis Smith, the third-shift guards on duty when the murders occurred.

"Dammit, Brandt! Henderson lives in far Southeast and Lewis is way out in Laurel, Maryland! Call them both right now and make sure they're home. I'll take Joe Henderson myself. I want to look that drunk in the face when he explains himself. Remember, Brandt, don't talk to anybody about where you're going or what you find out."

Back at the crime scene Matt questioned Earl Simms, the security guard who found the bodies.

"I understand the Canadian women were the first to see the bodies."

"Yes, sir. That's right. I was at my post at the Mall entrance when I heard all this commotion coming from in here. I ran back here to see what was going on. That's when I met those old women running out of here like bats out of hell. All of them were pretty upset; but one came back into the exhibit to show me the two dead men over there."

"What did the women tell you?"

"Not much. They said they were walking through the exhibit when they saw the bodies. They said they didn't hear any gunshots; and that everything was quiet and they were the only people in the exhibit. That's about it, lieutenant."

"What time did you get to work, today, Mr. Simms?"

"Same time I usually do, eight o'clock."

"Did you notice anything unusual when you arrived this morning?"

"Nope. Everything looked okay to me."

"So, who do you think killed them, Simms?"

"I don't know who coulda done something like that, lieutenant. Jesus Christ, what's the Smithsonian coming to when people get murdered right under our noses?"

"That's a good question, Mr. Simms. Has anyone on your staff identified the victims yet?"

"No sir. Nobody seems to know who they are or why they're dressed like that, either."

"They're obviously dressed to kill, Mr. Simms. No doubt about that. What do you make of those clothes?"

"You got me there, lieutenant."

"Is there anyone around here who knows anything for certain, Mr. Simms?"

"I don't know, sir," Earl Simms answered with a confused look on his face.

Matt watched Earl Simms walk away before turning his attention to the murder victims. They were both young, hardly past their teens. They were also short and dark skinned, with well defined biceps and strong, broad shoulders. They might have been brothers. Their faces were round and full, giving the impression of stockiness, despite lean, hard bodies.

The torso wound had bled profusely down the abdomen and left leg of the standing corpse, but there was less blood from the chest wound on the sitting body. The standing corpse retained some semblance of dignity, despite the swelling and discoloration of the face. But the body of his companion looked ridiculous, like a racist caricature of a black man, with its bulging eyes above a sagging jaw and grotesquely protruding tongue. Their exposed genitals were the final insult to young lives snuffed out far too soon.

Steve Mitchell joined Matt in front of the diorama. "Very unnatural crime scene for the Museum of Natural History."

"Tell me about it. They seem to get weirder by the day, Steve. Whatever happened to old-fashioned homicides where somebody takes you out for balling his wife or daughter?"

"Murder has to keep up with the times, my friend. This is a brave new world we're living in where the usual motives for murder don't cut it when you're up against cyberspace and virtual reality and saturation levels of violence everywhere you look. And people wonder why we're the most violent nation in the world."

"So we're left to mop up this bizarre crap because nobody else out there is minding the store. You remember how outraged people used to be when somebody committed a serial murder."

"Yeah, I remember when Richard Speck killed those nurses in Chicago. People couldn't believe that another human being could do something like that."

"Now serial murders are as common as a head cold. Manson, Bundy, Gacy, Son of Sam, Dahmer. What's happening to us, Steve?"

"My guess is the same thing that happened to Rome before it fell. What we're exposed to nowadays isn't a far cry from the spectacles they put on in the Coliseum."

Matt left Steve Mitchell and walked over to where Sam and the criminalists were lifting blood and other trace evidence from the crime scene."

"Steve says the bullets didn't exit the bodies, Sam.

What's your guess on the weapon?"

"Can't say for certain, but from the pattern of the splatter and the amount of blood loss, I'd say it was something small like a .22-caliber. Can't be sure, though."

Jake returned from his errand at the Castle.

"I couldn't find Kendricks, Matt. I went over to his office but he's not there. His secretary said he's supposed to be over here."

"Well, where's Brandt, the chief of security for this museum?" Matt asked.

"I checked downstairs, and he ain't in his office, either," Jake replied.

"So I'm supposed to believe that both of them have dropped off the face of the earth?"

Jake shrugged.

"Forget it, Jake. Where's the museum d irector."

"I do know where he is, partner. He went over to the Castle for a meeting with Secretary Marshall 30 minutes ago."

"Where's the secretary's office?"

"On the third floor."

Inside the Castle, the third-floor receptionist escorted Matt and Jake to Andrew Marshall's suite of offices, where they found his private secretary manning the barricades. She refused to interrupt his meeting or to allow them to enter the conference room where the meeting was being held.

They burst into the conference room anyway, bringing an abrupt halt to Marshall's meeting with his museum directors. The aide ran in after them. Everyone around the table stared raptly as she babbled excuses to Secretary Marshall, who had, by that time, risen from his seat and walked around the table to where the detectives were standing.

"It's okay, I'll handle it," Marshall insisted as he escorted his secretary out of the conference room and closed the door.

"I'm Andrew Marshall. To what do I owe this unexpected pleasure, gentlemen?"

"I'm Lieutenant Alexander, Mr. Marshall, and this is my partner, Sergeant Jackson. We're investigating your murders for you."

"I wouldn't exactly call them our murders, lieutenant. We know very little about the murders or the victims."

"So I've been told several times this morning. If you think I buy that, you probably have a bridge you want to sell me, next."

"We're not trying to sell you anything, Lieutenant Alexander," Secretary Marshall insisted as he went back to his seat.

"Where's Colonel Kendricks and Chief Brandt?" Matt demanded.

The secretary looked confused before directing his question to Fisher: "Aren't they in the museum, Bill?"

"They were over there when I left for your meeting, Andy."

"I just came from the museum, and they're not over there now," Matt insisted.

"Bill, will you take care of this?" the secretary asked.

Fisher looked annoyed and angry as he rose to leave.

"Not so fast, Mr. Marshall. So far, I've run into a brick wall every time I talk to one of your people. Nobody knows anything about the murder victims. Your security staff, who ought to know what the hell happened over there, disappear before our eyes, and your office staff tries to keep me from talking to you."

"My secretary was just doing her job, lieutenant. It was nothing personal."

"I take murder very personally, Mr. Marshall. I'm sure the murder victims took it personally, too, when someone at your museum snuffed them last night."

"You have no evidence that anyone in Natural History killed those men!" Fisher shouted. "No one on my staff had anything to do with the murders."

"Why would the victims be cooling their heels in your museum, if everybody on your staff is as pure as the driven snow? Don't think because the murders occurred at the almighty Smithsonian Institution you can roll over us with a wall of high class bullshit. I'm trying to be nice, but I can close that mother of a museum down and search every inch of it if I want to, and that ought to take about four weeks, minimum. I can also fix it so the press will be swarming all over this place in less than 30 minutes. It's up to you."

Andrew Marshall frowned before replying, "We're overworked and understaffed, Lieutenant Alexander. Wally Kendricks is responsible for security at a dozen Smithsonian sites in the District. If you can't find him, he's probably at one of the other sites. I told my senior staff to give you all the cooperation you need; and I'll be here anytime you need to talk to me. I think you already know the way to my office."

Matt looked unconvinced as he and Jake followed Fisher out of the conference room and back across the Mall to the Museum of Natural History.

With a worried look, Secretary Marshall watched the two detectives leave.

"Paul, close the door, please."

Paul Davis, Director of the Arts and Industry Museum, quickly moved to the door and back to his seat among the five other directors of museums on the Mall.

"We have a real problem, people."

"The murders couldn't have happened at a worse time, Andy," agreed Robert Engels, Director of the Museum of American History. "The budget hearings for the next fiscal year are in full swing and they aren't going well. I thought the *Enola Gay* exhibit was history, but the committee members managed to drag that up again."

"I know exactly what you mean, Bob," Ailene Parham, Director of the Freer Gallery of Art, replied. "The House committee skewered Herb last week. I was next in line to testify on my budget, and I'm telling you it was pure torture sitting there while they pounded Herb into the ground. I never saw such penny-pinching, nitpicking over a budget. The atmosphere was so adversarial you could have cut it with a knife."

"Ailene is right. I knew I was in for a rough time; but they put me through hell, especially Chairman Harris," said Herbert Vaughan, director of the National Air and Space Museum. "They won't let up on the *Enola Gay*. As far as I'm concerned, that controversy is dead and buried; but they keep digging it up and rubbing our faces in it. I've got battle scars from my testimony, Andy."

"There's no question that these hearings are the most hostile we've experienced since I became secretary. I thought we were already at rock bottom on the Hill, but these murders have proved me wrong. Once Chairman Harris finds out, we'll be finished up there as far as any budget increase is concerned. Who's left to testify?"

"I'm scheduled for tomorrow at two," replied Bernard Wampler, Director of the Hirshorn Museum and Sculpture Garden. "That Lieutenant Alexander is going to be a major pain in the ass, Andy. Isn't there anything we can do about him?"

"Why don't you research that one for me, Bernie. Find out if we can use any of our contacts in the District government to shorten his leash a bit. It looks like he's not going to cut us any slack, and we need all the help we can get to contain the fallout from these murders."

"I'll get started on that as soon as I get back to my office."

"Does anybody know what happened at Natural History?" asked Ailene Parham.

"You know everything I know, Ailene; and you saw that Bill didn't know as much as I did," the secretary replied. "As far as we know, the men who were murdered are perfect strangers. They didn't work here, and no one admits knowing them."

"Isn't it strange that they would be dressed in ritual attire? Why would anyone dress up like African warriors and break into Natural History? What could they have been doing over there?" Ailene asked as Secretary Marshall rose to adjourn the meeting. After the secretary left, the museum directors lingered in his conference room, discussing the murders.

Back at the Museum of Natural History, Matt checked in at the crime scene while Fisher looked for his errant security chief, Willis Brandt, with Jake close on his heels. Steve Mitchell asked Matt if he wanted to sit in on the autopsies. Matt agreed and Steve promised to call to let him know when they were scheduled.

"Don't lose anything this time, Mitchell," Sam shouted after the Deputy Medical Examiner as Steve Mitchell struggled with one end of the second body bag.

"I've told you a hundred times we didn't lose those panties, Sam. They were in that bag with the rest of her clothes when they left the lab."

"That's a lie and you know it. One of you panty-stealing freaks in the Medical Examiner's office stole those drawers. They weren't in with her other clothes. You knew that when you sent them over."

Steve stopped in front of Matt, who was laughing along with Lois and Ruby, Sam's forensic specialists.

"Why does he bring that up every time he sees me?"

"Sam is real particular about his work, Steve. He took it personal when those panties went missing."

"The District prosecutor still got a conviction without the panties. That rapist went down for life. You'd think Sam would be satisfied."

"Sam won't be satisfied until those panties turn up,"

Matt laughed after Steve wobbled toward the elevator holding one end of the second body bag.

"Where'd Bryant go? Sam?"

"How the hell do I know where he went? He got a telephone call and left. Said he had a meeting."

"Meeting nothing. He's just ducking out of work as usual. Find anything interesting?"

"You might want to take a look in one of those leather pouches over there."

Sam motioned toward his evidence bags, which had been placed in a box on the perimeter of the crime scene.

Matt donned a pair of plastic gloves. When he opened the first evidence bag, he found a small leather pouch with nothing more than a small quantity of gray dust clinging to the inside. When he opened the second bag, a gorgeous, shimmering, intensely green, breathtakingly beautiful emerald necklace tumbled out of yet another leather pouch, caught the light, and curled snake-like across the toe of his right shoe.

"Now, that's something worth dying for," Matt concluded. "Who else knows about this necklace, Sam?"

"Just you and me, Alexander. Just you and me. You want to keep it that way?" Sam asked, laughing.

"Damn! Look at the size of these emeralds! You think it's real, Sam?"

"If they are real, they're the biggest damned emeralds I ever laid eyes on."

"Well, I guess we know why they were killed."

"If they were killed for the emeralds, why didn't the shooter take the necklace? Doesn't make sense that they'd still have it on them."

"Maybe he didn't have time."

"Didn't have anything but time. Those stiffs had been in this exhibit for well over 10 hours when their bodies were found."

"Give me one of those plastic bags, Sam."

"Where the hell do you think you're going with my evidence?"

"To find out where this necklace came from. I'll be in the museum director's office if you need me."

Matt ran into Jake in the rotunda, where he learned that Kendricks and Brandt were still missing. Jake also told him that both Kendricks and Brandt had gone into Brandt's office two hours earlier, that they hadn't stayed in the office long, and that they both had left the museum shortly afterwards.

"It's 10 past four, Jake. We need to get started taking statements from the security guards on duty this morning. But right now I'm going upstairs to talk to Fisher about a pricey little item Sam found on one of the bodies."

Matt lifted the plastic bag holding the necklace out of his pocket and showed it to Jake.

"Have mercy! Are they real?"

"I'll soon find out," Matt replied as he left Jake on his way to the museum director's office.

CHAPTER 3

Bill Fisher looked anxious when Matt entered his plush office in the Museum of Natural History.

"What can you tell me about this, Fisher?" Matt asked as he dropped the emerald necklace on Fisher's desk."

"Where did you get this necklace?" Fisher demanded.

"Our forensic specialist took it off one of the murder victims. Don't take it out of the bag. It may have some trace evidence on it."

Fisher jumped up from his desk and ran out of his office, still holding the necklace.

"Hey, wait a minute. Where do you think you're going with my evidence?"

"Over to the gem collection. This necklace is supposed to be on display in a theft-proof case."

Matt followed close on Fisher's heels as the Director rushed through the corridors leading to the gem exhibit and over to the case where the necklace should have been displayed. Fisher stopped dead in his tracks when he found an identical emerald necklace reclining on a bed of supple black velvet, its brilliant green color shimmering from the subtle lighting inside the case. Both necklaces looked absolutely genuine.

"What's going on, Fisher?"

"Dammit!" is all Fisher uttered before he led Matt into the suite of staff offices behind the gem collection.

Fisher hurried down the narrow corridor with offices on both sides until he reached a door with the name *Henry Hughes, Chief Curator, Precious and Semi-Precious Stones.* Fisher burst into the office and threw the necklace he was carrying onto the desk in front of Henry Hughes. Startled by the sudden intrusion into his office, Hughes jumped up from his desk.

"What the hell is this, Henry?"

"It's the tumbled emerald necklace from our collection."

"Wrong, Henry. Our necklace is still in its case. Where did this necklace come from?"

"I don't know what you're talking about, Bill. What's going on?" Hughes asked as he held the plastic bag containing the necklace up to the light.

"Can you tell whether this necklace is genuine or fake?" Matt asked Henry Hughes.

"Of course he can tell if it's a fake," Fisher replied. "He's our gem expert."

Henry Hughes opened the plastic bag to take the necklace out.

"You can't touch it with your hands," Matt cautioned. "We took this necklace off one of the murder victims; and there may be evidence on the stones."

"How can I examine this necklace it if I can't touch it, lieutenant?"

"You'll have to do the best you can, Henry," Fisher insisted. I need to know what's going on around here.

First two murders and now this necklace. I need some damned answers, quick."

Hughes looked skeptical as he sat down and turned on a bright lamp over his desk. He lifted the necklace out of the plastic envelope with a large pair of tweezers and looked at one of the stones under a microscope. He looked puzzled when he finished his examination.

"You said this was found on one of the murder victims?"

"Yeah, that's right," Matt replied.

Hughes switched his computer on and inserted a CD-ROM disk. Then he opened a file from the disk on the gem collection's tumbled emerald necklace. Matt walked behind the desk to get a better view of the computer screen. Fisher followed suit. Hughes scrolled through several screens until he found a diagram of the necklace with all of the emeralds numbered. He matched a corresponding stone on the necklace to one of the numbered stones in the diagram and typed "inclusions" on the screen. The computer called up a photograph of the particular stone with a map of its imperfections. Hughes alternated between examining the computer map and the stone. He finally looked up frowning, clearly unhappy with what he had seen in the stone.

"A first-rate emerald can have enough inclusions to make a diamond worthless. Inclusions are important, though, because they occur naturally, and it's damned near impossible to fake them. They can also tell you where the stone came from. I need to take this necklace to my laboratory, Bill."

"I'll have to go with you," Matt insisted. "That necklace is an important piece of evidence, and I can't let it out of my sight."

"That's fine by me, lieutenant," Hughes replied as he led the way down the corridor to his laboratory.

"Everybody in the museum is on edge, Bill," Hughes said as they walked to his lab. "They know about the murders, but they don't know who's been killed or who killed them. It seems to me that someone ought to brief the staff about what's going on."

"I don't need you to tell me my job, Henry. I hit the ground running this morning, and I've been up against it ever since. I've had meetings with Col. Kendricks, the museum's security staff, the Park Police, the secretary, and Lieutenant Alexander. I'll get around to the staff on my time," Fisher replied, fairly bristling at the suggestion that he was not on top of the situation.

Once they got to the lab, Matt watched as Hughes prepared his scientific instruments for testing the necklace. Fisher lost interest in the testing as he paced, brooding, back and forth near the laboratory's door. Hughes explained the equipment he was using to Matt including their obscure sounding names and parts that Matt struggled to spell as he took notes.

"This is a refractometer, which is used to establish the refractive index of a gem stone. If I know what the specific gravity of the stone is, I can use that plus the refractive index to identify the stone."

"Well, is it genuine?" Fisher demanded.

"I'll tell you after I look at it under the polarizing

microscope," Hughes said as he turned the microscope on.

"Emeralds are more valuable than diamonds, second only to rubies, actually. It used to be that only a beryl colored by Chromium was considered a genuine emerald; but now beryls colored by Vanadium are also accepted as emeralds. The best emeralds have always come from the Chivor and Muzo mines in Colombia. Muzo has produced emeralds as large as 300 carats each. Some of Muzo's best emeralds are in the crown jewels of Iran. Maharajahs and Sheiks of the Ottoman Empire also coveted Muzo's stones. They're the world's standard. Sometimes Jadeite or Olivine are passed off as emeralds because of their intensely green color; but both stones are more dense than emeralds and Olivine is doubly refractive, what we call birefringent. When a light ray enters olivine, it's normally split into two polarized light waves, each with its own refractive index. Let's see if the light splits."

Matt and Bill Fisher crowded around the microscope as Henry Hughes placed the necklace under the microscope. Hughes isolated one stone and focused the light through it. He rotated the stone very slowly. The polarized light didn't split.

"Well that's the last test, Bill. It's the genuine tumbled emerald necklace, all right," Hughes said as he put the necklace back into the plastic bag. "I knew that when I looked at the inclusions under the microscope. They were too similar for it to be a fake. These tests simply confirmed the fact."

"How did this necklace get out of its case, Henry? And how in God's name did a fake get in there?"

"Considering the security system for the gem collection, I'd say it was physically impossible for anyone to have stolen this necklace if I weren't holding it in my hand," Hughes replied.

"When was the last time the system was tested?" Fisher asked.

"Six months ago. But there's absolutely no indication that anyone breached the security system last night."

"That's all very well, but the necklace was stolen anyway!" Fisher roared. "How am I supposed to explain this to the secretary? Two murders and a major theft all in the same night. This is too much, Henry! Too damned much!"

"I still need to examine the necklace in the case, Bill," Hughes insisted as he returned the genuine necklace to Fisher. "Nobody could have gotten this necklace out of its case without tripping the security system. You know we put in three backups to the system. I swear it's foolproof."

"Looks like we're the fools, Henry. Get that other necklace and test it right now. If it's really a fake, some damned heads are going to roll around here, starting with Kendricks and his good-for-nothing security guards."

"If this necklace was stolen from its case, our forensics specialist will have to process that crime scene for evidence, too," Matt added.

Henry Hughes' handsome face looked strained as he locked his laboratory and walked back to his office to call security to initiate the protocol for opening the computerized locks to the display cases in the gem collection.

"The security system for the gem collection has been in place for five years, Bill. We paid over $5 million dollars for that system, and we've never had a problem with it before."

"Something is very wrong," Fisher replied.

"I'll take that necklace now that you're finished with it, Fisher," Matt insisted.

"Where are you going to take it?" Fisher demanded.

"When I leave here, I'm taking it downtown to the DCPD Property Division, and I'm going to log it in as evidence in this homicide investigation."

"You can't take that necklace out of the museum!" both Fisher and Hughes shouted at the same time.

"That necklace is priceless, lieutenant. It's one of a kind, and it contains the largest emeralds in our collection. Besides that, we can't protect the necklace if it leaves the museum," Fisher protested.

"You couldn't protect it here, Fisher. We'll keep it under lock and key," Matt insisted.

Fisher's face grew red as he stared Matt down and stood his ground.

"This necklace leaves this museum over my dead body, lieutenant!"

"That's easily arranged, Fisher, considering you have a homicidal maniac running around loose in here."

"The necklace is insured for $10 million, Lieutenant Alexander. Can the Police Department replace it if it's stolen?" Henry Hughes calmly inquired.

Matt heard the clear voice of reason as he contemplated the shit that would hit the fan if the necklace disappeared while in police custody.

"Once the necklace leaves the Smithsonian, our insurance company no longer covers it, so the city will be liable for any damage or theft that occurs while it's in your custody," Hughes continued.

"We have a serious problem here," Matt explained. "This necklace is a major piece of evidence in my homicide investigation. That means our forensics specialist has to examine it; and that we have to establish a chain of custody for it. How can we do that if you keep the necklace in the museum?"

"We'll have to figure something out, because this necklace can't leave the Smithsonian," Fisher insisted as he and Matt followed Henry Hughes back to the gem exhibit.

Kendricks, Chief Brandt, and Sam Johnson, the homicide division's forensic specialist, were waiting for them at the exhibit. Sam told them not to touch the door to the exhibit as he quickly dusted it for prints.

"Fancy meeting the two of you here," Matt said. "I thought you and Brandt had taken the rest of the day off, Kendricks."

"Chief Brandt and I had some emergency business to attend to at one of the museums off the Mall, lieutenant. We got back as soon as we could."

"I was born yesterday, Kendricks; but I stayed awake all night," Matt replied, his voice heavy with sarcasm.

Sam looked curious, but said nothing.

Brandt looked scared, but Kendricks showed no discomfort in looking Matt straight in the face and lying to him about where they had been.

"It looks like there was a goddamned free-for-all in the museum last night, Kendricks," Fisher shouted. "Two murders and now a priceless emerald necklace stolen. What do you have to say for yourself?"

"I don't know what you're talking about, Fisher."

"This necklace says you're the one who doesn't know what you're talking about," Fisher shouted as he snatched the necklace from Henry Hughes and shoved it in Kendricks' face. "Those men stole one of the best pieces in our gem collection before they were killed last night."

"That's a lie, Fisher. Nobody broke into the gem exhibit last night."

"Can we dispense with the debate and get this over with?" Matt demanded as he retrieved the necklace from Fisher, who was extremely reluctant to let it go.

Willis Brandt quickly punched his code into the keypad at the door leading into the exhibit cases. He was followed by Kendricks and Hughes. After the door released its locking mechanism, Sam insisted that everyone wait outside as he examined the narrow corridor behind the cases for trace evidence. Fisher nearly died of apoplexy waiting for Sam to finish. Then they all entered the narrow corridor behind the display cases. The door closed behind them and locked automatically immediately after it shut.

"Which one of the cases do you want opened?" Brandt asked.

"Number seven," Hughes replied. Sam then proceeded to dust the case, after which they began the same process on the computer keypad attached to the case. Brandt and Kendricks used the same codes, but Hughes entered a new code which varied for each of the cases. The door on the back of the case popped open to reveal a sophisticated combination lock, which Henry Hughes opened from memory. Visitors in front of the case watched incredulously as Hughes extracted the necklace, which Sam placed in a plastic evidence bag.

Hughes carried the second necklace as the entourage made its way back to his laboratory where he examined the necklace from the case on the refractometer with Brandt, Kendricks, Matt, and Fisher looking on. Hughes then took the necklace over to the polarizing microscope. He adjusted the light on the microscope and rotated the selected stone until the light split.

"It's a fake."

"What kind of security system are you running, Kendricks? Do you know how bad this makes me look?" Fisher shouted.

"Get off my back, Fisher! I tried to fire Joe Henderson's drunken butt; but you stepped in and pulled his fat out of the fire not once, but twice. How can I secure this site when fifty percent of the security staff on third-shift shows up drunk every night? You've only got yourself to blame!"

"I'll be damned if I take the fall for your incompetence, Kendricks. This is your fault! You're Director of Security."

"It is not my fault! I begged the budget committee not to cut my staff. All of you know goddamned well I can't protect these sites without trained staff."

"It's just like you to blame your staff for your own incompetence."

"That's enough, Fisher. If you say another word I'll kick your fat white ass from one end of this laboratory to the other," Kendricks threatened as he made a menacing move toward Fisher.

Fisher stood his ground, but held his tongue. Matt, Hughes, and Brandt stood uncomfortably around the lab, pretending that they hadn't heard a word. Hughes was the first to speak.

"What should we do about this fake, Bill?"

"We have to put the fake back into the case, Henry, so we don't arouse suspicion."

"And just what do you intend doing with the genuine necklace?" Matt asked.

"I'll let you know after I talk to Secretary Marshall, lieutenant. I can't authorize doing anything with the necklace without his permission."

"Both of these necklaces are material evidence in my homicide investigation. Let's go over to the secretary's office right now so we can get some closure on this today, Fisher."

Kendricks sent Willis Brandt over to the secretary's office with Matt and Fisher. Fisher looked as edgy as a bull in a china shop when they were shown into Andrew

Marshall's private office. The three of them sat in thickly upholstered Chippendale chairs at a large mahogany table to one side of the secretary's spacious office.

"To what do I owe this dubious pleasure, gentlemen?" Secretary Marshall asked as he walked into the office from his conference room.

Fisher took the necklace out of his pocket and dropped it on the table.

"Isn't this piece from our collection, Bill?"

"It's one of our best pieces. It was on display in the gem exhibit until last night."

"So why have you brought it to my office?"

"We found this necklace on one of the homicide victims," Matt replied.

"It was stolen from its case in the gem exhibit, Andy; and a fake was left in its place," Fisher softly added while avoiding eye contact with the secretary.

The secretary sat upright, leaned forward, and stared Fisher straight in the face.

"Bill, are you telling me that someone broke into the gem exhibit and stole this necklace?"

"They must have, Andy. Henry Hughes says the necklace on display in the case is a fake. This is the authentic tumbled emerald necklace from our collection, Andy," Fisher insisted, pointing to the emerald necklace lying in the middle of the table; and it was found on one of the murdered men."

"You're asking me to believe that two men broke into the museum, got past security, and stole this necklace out of the most sophisticated state-of-the-art security system money can buy?"

"I don't know how they stole the necklace, Andy. Both Kendricks and Henry Hughes swear there hasn't been any breach in security for the gem exhibit. But they must have gotten in there, because here's the necklace."

"Two murders and the theft of the most expensive piece in our gem collection. Just how the hell am I supposed to explain all this to the board, Bill?"

Fisher was sweating profusely as he stammered, "I don't know, Andy. I just don't know."

"Where's Kendricks?"

"I left him with Henry Hughes."

Andrew Marshall called his secretary and told her to get Kendricks over to his office immediately.

"Lieutenant Alexander wants to take both necklaces with him. He says they have to be kept under police custody."

"That's right, Mr. Secretary. We have to establish a chain of custody for all the evidence we collect in a homicide investigation. Both necklaces are crucial pieces of evidence."

"I'm sorry, lieutenant, but you can't take this necklace away from the museum. You should never have brought it over here without proper security."

"Let's resolve this right now," Matt insisted. "Our forensics specialist has to examine each necklace for prints, blood, fiber, and trace evidence. He can't examine them if we can't have access to them."

"We have laboratories here at the Smithsonian that he can use."

Barbara Fleming

"That doesn't solve the problem of the chain of custody. The District prosecutor will have to take all the evidence we found at the crime scene to trial and testify to who's had access to it between the murders and the trial. He can't do that if you keep the necklaces at the museum."

"We can't allow this necklace to be taken out of the museum, Lieutenant Alexander. The risk of theft is too high."

"If it stays here, I want our forensics expert to examine the necklace before he leaves today; and I want you, Mr. Marshall, to personally guarantee that the necklace will remain in your custody until the trial."

"I'll talk to Kendricks about the best way to protect the necklace when he gets here. Get both necklaces examined by their forensics specialist first thing, Bill. I want the genuine necklace back under lock and key as soon as possible."

Matt, Fisher, and Brandt returned to the Museum of Natural History at six o'clock. Matt stopped in at the crime scene to inform Sam about the arrangements for examining the necklace. Ruby and Lois watched the ensuing fireworks from a safe distance.

"How the hell do you expect me to work without my equipment, Alexander?"

"The lab they want you to use here has plenty of equipment, Sam."

"That's bullshit, man. I need my own fucking equipment."

"Give me a break, Sam! They aren't going to let us

take the freaking necklaces out of the museum. I'm trying to cut a deal that will let you get the evidence off both necklaces. If you can do any better, be my guest!" Matt shouted in Sam's face.

"It's our goddamned evidence. Since when do we have to ask permission to take our own evidence back to the crime lab?"

"This particular evidence happens to be located on a $10 million necklace, Sam. Are you willing to take responsibility for the necklace after it leaves here?" Matt shouted.

"It's insured for $10 million, lieutenant. It's worth at least three or four times that much," Fisher insisted. "Actually, it's priceless, considering its age."

"So, it's the real deal, huh?" Sam asked in a chastened voice.

"Yes, it's real, Sam. Any more questions?"

"I'll have to bring my equipment over here. Where's the lab?"

"Fisher will take you over there."

Matt turned to Willis Brandt after Sam and Fisher left.

"This crime scene needs to be secured. I don't want anyone in here until we release it. I also need an office where I can question staff, Brandt."

"You can use my assistant's office. He's on vacation. It's next door to my office."

Matt and Brandt left for the lower level of the museum and entered Chief Brandt's office. Brandt poured coffee for Matt and himself.

"Seems like I've spent the entire day running in circles, Brandt. Why do I get the feeling that you people are trying to do an end run around my investigation?"

"I don't know what you mean, lieutenant."

"I think you do. Two murders and a major jewel heist, and you've been blowing smoke up my ass all day. You and Kendricks disappear for nearly four hours this morning; and you lie about where you've been after you get back."

"We weren't lying," Brandt protested as a warm flush crept up his face, turning his pink freckles red.

"I think you're still lying; but let's change the subject to the murder victims and how they got into the museum. What did you find when you checked to see if there had been a break-in last night?"

"Everything was locked down tighter than a drum. I don't know how those men got in here, but they didn't force their way in."

"We didn't find anything during our search, either."

"Nobody broke in here last night, lieutenant."

"There you go again, Brandt. Are you certain they didn't work here?"

"Absolutely, but that's not to say they never worked here. I'd have to know their social security numbers to check our old personnel files."

"They weren't carrying any identification, so I guess that's out of the question for now," Matt concluded. "I have to question all the security guards who had anything to do with finding the bodies before they leave the museum, Brandt. I also need the two guards who were on duty during third-shift back in here."

"They don't come on duty until midnight."

"I'm having them picked up, so I need their addresses."

"The security staff is already raising hell about staying late, lieutenant."

"Too bad. Tell them if they leave before they're questioned, I'll have them arrested, and they can tell me what I need to know from a jail cell."

Matt went into the office next door to Brandt's and waited for him to return with the security staff. He used the time to go over the day's events.

Two unidentified murdered men, a priceless emerald necklace stolen and recovered, a collective case of amnesia about the murders by the museum staff, and a classic cover-up by the Smithsonian's administrative staff. The first order of business would be to identify the victims. Matt was convinced that someone at the Smithsonian knew the victims, despite their denials. He was also convinced that it would be damned difficult to establish a motive for murder without knowing who the victims were or whether anyone at the Smithsonian had a prior relationship with them. The most obvious scenario for the murders pointed to the third-shift security guards. It was logical that they might have shot two intruders trying to steal the emerald necklace. But finding both bodies in the diorama the following morning shot that premise to hell. If the guards had killed them, they would have reported it immediately; and they would not have left the bodies in the diorama overnight.

Matt looked up as Jake walked through the door.

"Everything's taken care of upstairs. What's next?" Jake asked.

"I want you to pick up the guards who were on third-shift duty last night. Here are their names and addresses."

"It's looking like a long night, partner."

"The sooner we start, the sooner we finish, man."

Brandt returned with Earl Simms and several of the day-shift guards trailing him down the corridor as Jake left.

"There were over 20 guards on duty during the day-shift, lieutenant. Simms was the first person to find the victims."

"I talked to Simms briefly this morning. Send him in."

CHAPTER 4

Earl Simms entered the office warily. Matt motioned for him to sit in one of the two armchairs facing the desk.

"Who was in the museum when you arrived this morning, Simms?"

"The third-shift guards were leaving, so it was just first-shift security, maintenance, and housekeeping."

"What about the security console out there?"

"Chief Brandt assigns one person from each shift to man the console. We rotate on it because it's a lot of boring work, and nobody likes sitting there all the time."

"Do the cameras run all night?"

"We run all the cameras until midnight. After midnight, we just run the cameras covering entrances, exits, and stairs. Then we take the video tapes out of the console. . ."

"Wait a minute! Are you telling me that video tapes were made off the cameras running in this museum last night?" Matt asked in disbelief.

"As far as I know there were," Earl answered in confusion. "Didn't they tell you about the video tapes?"

"You know damned well they didn't tell me about any damned video tapes, Simms! Matt shouted as he stormed out of his office and burst into Willis Brandt's.

"Where're the tapes, Brandt?"

"What tapes?"

"You know damned well what tapes! The video tapes that were made on your security system last night."

"They should be in the security console where we keep them."

"Why didn't you tell me you had the tapes before now?"

"I've had a lot on my mind today, lieutenant."

"I don't see how something as important as that could slip your mind. Seems to me the tapes would be the first place you would look to find out what happened in here last night. Get Kendricks over here, now!"

Brandt rang Kendricks on his portable telephone as he escorted Matt to the security console manned by a middle-aged female guard. She was surprised at the sudden interest in her workstation. Brandt told her to show Matt the tapes that were made the previous day. She looked curious when she heard the request, but did as she was told.

"So you keep tapes from all the cameras?"

"Yes, that's right. We send them up to the video library. They keep them for 30 days and then we reuse them," the guard replied.

"How many cameras do you keep on after midnight?"

"Ten cameras run all night."

"I need those third-shift tapes, Brandt. The Deputy Medical Examiner says the victims probably died between one and three o'clock this morning."

"I can't give you permission to take the tapes," Brandt

insisted as Kendricks walked up on their conversation. "He wants to take all of the tapes that were made on third-shift, sir."

"It's our policy to review the tapes ourselves whenever there's been a major incident in the museum; and we don't have any backups of yesterday's tapes," Kendricks replied.

"Do you honestly expect me to believe you haven't looked at these tapes already, Kendricks? You had plenty of time when you disappeared for four hours today."

"I don't know what you're talking about, lieutenant."

"It's your wagon, Kendricks, but I want those damned tapes now. I'll get a warrant if you force me to."

The security guard began retrieving the third-shift tapes from the bin under the security console and placing them in a plastic bag.

"Oh yeah, I forgot to tell you that the sign-in log from third-shift is missing, too, lieutenant," Brandt said.

"What sign-in log?"

"Staff are supposed to sign in if they stay in the museum after closing hours. We use logs on second and third-shifts so we can keep track of who's in the museum after it closes. Wilbur Daniels entered the sign-in log for the second-shift into the computer at the end of his shift last night; but the log for the third-shift wasn't entered in the computer, and it's missing."

"Who was responsible for the log?" Matt asked

"Joe Henderson, when he's not drunk or asleep," Kendricks derisively answered.

"So what you're telling me is that you don't know who

was in the museum after midnight."

"We know the security guards were here, but we don't know whether any other staff members were here," Kendricks replied.

"Yeah, right. How many staff people work in this museum, Kendricks?"

"About 200 employees at this site."

"And nobody knows who the hell was in here during third-shift?" Matt asked, not expecting an answer as the female security guard handed him the bag of video tapes. "Man, you people blow more smoke than Forty going north," Matt insisted as he took the tapes and left Kendricks and Brandt standing at the camera console watching his retreat.

The security guards waiting outside the assistant director's office all demanded to know how much longer they'll have to wait. Matt ignored them. Earl Simms' nerves hadn't improved while waiting for Matt to return.

"When we talked before, you said you didn't see or hear anything unusual this morning, Simms."

"Not until I heard those Canadian women screaming."

"Did you see the third-shift guards when you came on duty this morning?"

"Yeah, I saw Lewis checking out as I was coming in, and I passed Joe at the security console. Joe can't leave the console until his replacement on day shows up, so he was still sitting there when I passed through on my way to the elevators."

"How were Smith and Henderson behaving?"

"They didn't act like anything was wrong to me."

"What time did you hear the women screaming at the murder scene?"

"It must have been around 10 o'clock. That's when all hell broke loose in here."

"Are you certain the Canadian women were the first ones to see the bodies?"

"If somebody else saw them, they didn't report it to me. Seeing as how the men had been shot dead and had their privates exposed like that, I think anybody else would have reported it pretty fast, lieutenant."

"What happened after you found the bodies?"

"Well, all that commotion from the Canadian women raised a crowd, but they were mainly staff people and guards. Janice from the information desk ran back there and fainted dead away. They had to carry her to the ladies' restroom. Then I called Chief Brandt and he called Col. Kendricks."

"I need you to list the names of all the people who you remember being in the exhibit, Simms," Matt said as he handed Earl a pad and pencil.

"I might not remember all of them, lieutenant."

"Well, list the ones you do remember. I understand you were the first person to look at the bodies close up."

"Yeah, that's right. I had to walk through the diorama to get a good look."

"You're a trained security guard, Simms. Don't you know better than to go trampling through a crime scene like that?"

"I just wanted to get a closer look at the bodies, lieutenant, to see if it was any of our employees."

"Are you sure you didn't tamper with anything while you were in there?"

"I swear I didn't touch a thing. Col. Kendricks asked me to feel the bodies to see if they were cold, but I wouldn't. He had to do it himself."

"Kendricks, too, huh? Looks like there was a regular free-for-all at the crime scene. Did you see him tamper with any evidence?"

"No, he just felt the bodies and left."

"Are you sure you don't know those men, Simms?"

"No, sir. I've never seen them before in my life."

Matt questioned Earl Simms for several more minutes. When he finished, he asked Earl to send the next guard in on his way out. Earl handed Matt the list of names before he left. Matt looked grim when he saw how many names were on the list.

"Where is that snitch Henry Bryant when I need him?" Matt mumbled to himself as he followed Simms out of the office and handed Simms' list of names to Brandt.

"Keep the guards whose names are on that list and let the rest of them go home, Brandt. I'll catch up with them tomorrow."

"At least nine of the guards are on this list. At the rate you're going, we'll be here all night."

"Let me worry about that, Brandt. My partner should be back soon."

"Col. Kendricks told me to stay until you finish. How much longer are you going to be?"

"As long as it takes, Brandt. As long as it takes."

Brandt gave Matt a disgusted look and returned to his office just as Jake arrived with Joe Henderson and Lewis Smith, the third-shift security guards in tow.

"Got your men," Jake said.

"That didn't take long," Matt replied.

"Got some help with Smith. I picked up Henderson myself."

"Jake, you take Smith in Brandt's office until I finish with Henderson. Then we both need to get started on the guards outside."

"Looks like quite a crowd," Jake ruefully admitted as he looked through the open door to the guards milling about in the first floor corridor.

"Tell me about it. Close the door on your way out, man."

"Sit down, Mr. Henderson."

Joe Henderson peered at Matt through very leery, permanently bloodshot eyes that gave his middle-aged face a haggard, seen-better-days look. Matt introduced himself to break the ice, but Henderson didn't warm to the bait.

"How long you gonna be, lieutenant? It's just about six o'clock and I have to be to work at midnight. I got business to take care of."

The look Matt gave Joe said they both knew that Joe's business was at the corner bar; but Joe defiantly held Matt's gaze as if to say "So what?"

"What time did you get to work last night, Henderson?"

"I was a little late relieving Wilbur Daniels."

"How late is a little late?"

"I probly got here 'round twelve twenty," Joe replied, stretching the truth in his favor.

"Tell me about the third-shift sign-in log."

"What about it?"

"Did you enter it into the computer before you left this morning?"

"Nah, I didn't enter it."

"Why not?"

"'Cause I couldn't find no log sheets to put out last night."

"So, you're saying there is no third-shift sign-in log."

"I tole you I couldn't find the log sheets."

"Chief Brandt didn't have any trouble finding them this morning."

"All I know is, I looked everywhere for them log sheets last night, and they wasn't nowhere to be found."

"Probably pissy drunk," Matt thought. "Did any staff people enter or leave the museum during third-shift?"

"Nah. I didn't see nobody."

"But you can't say for certain, can you, Henderson?"

"All I know is, I didn't see nobody leave last night, and I didn't let nobody in."

"Did you notice anything unusual during your shift?"

"Nah, everything was okay. Ask Lewis Smith. He was making rounds last night; and nothing happened."

"Two men were murdered during your shift, Henderson. It ought to be obvious to a blind man that everything was not okay in here last night."

"They wasn't murdered during my shift. I told Col.

Kendricks the same thing when he asked me 'bout it today."

"When did you talk to Col. Kendricks?" Matt asked.

"Ah . . . Ah . . . Shit! I talked to him earlier today. He came out to my house and asked me the same things you asking."

Matt gave Joe Henderson a hard look before resuming his questions.

"The medical examiner says the homicide victims were probably shot between one and three o'clock this morning. You were on the security console, Henderson. You must have seen something on your monitors."

"I didn't see nor hear nothing, and that's the God's honest truth."

"The question is why you didn't see or hear anything, Henderson, when two men were shot down like dogs in here. Did you leave the security console last night?"

"Yeah, I left. You don't expect me to sit all night without using the men's room, do you?"

Matt felt the question was moot, considering that Henderson had certainly topped off his bladder before coming to work.

"When did you go to the restroom?"

"I didn't keep track, but I guess I must a gone 'bout three or four times."

"So, someone could have entered or left the museum while you were in the bathroom?"

"Nah, nobody could come in because they woulda had to ring the buzzer at the staff entrance to get in after closing. Nobody rang the buzzer."

"But someone already inside could have left while you were in the bathroom. Or someone from inside could have let someone else in if you weren't at the security console. Isn't that so, Henderson?"

"Yeah, it coulda happened that way. "

"Or someone with a key to the staff entrance could have let themselves into the museum while you were in the men's room."

"There ain't no key to the staff entrance. You hafta punch a code into a keypad to open the door from the outside; but just a few people got that code. Everybody else hasta ring the buzzer after closing."

"So, how many people have that code?"

"Director Fisher, Chief Brandt, Col. Kendricks, and one guard on the evening and night-shifts. Lewis Smith has the code on third-shift. You have to use your PIN with the code before the door will open, though."

"So, the bottom line is, you don't know who the hell was in the museum during third-shift last night, do you, Henderson?"

"I'm telling you, nobody was in here last night. I woulda seen them on the monitors, and I ain't seen nobody last night. I go to the restroom every night, and nobody's been murdered before while I was taking a leak."

"But two people were murdered last night, Henderson."

"Maybe Wilbur Daniels let 'em in during second-shift. I know for a fact I didn't let nobody in last night."

"What time did you clock out this morning?"

"Right afta eight o'clock."

"Did you leave the museum right away?"

"Yeah. I didn't have no reason to stick 'round here."

"I don't have any more questions for now, Henderson; but I'll follow-up with you later."

"You found out who killed em?"

"I wouldn't be questioning you if I had."

"Bodies still here?"

"No, they're gone." Matt replied as he rose to escort Joe Henderson out of the office.

While he was out in the corridor, Matt stopped at the security console and asked Wilbur Daniels, the second-shift guard, to give him a copy of the sign-in log for the second-shift on Tuesday, the previous day. Wilbur quickly pulled it up on the computer and printed a copy. Matt studied the names on the list as he walked back to the office. He stopped in Brandt's office to let Jake know that he was ready to question Lewis Smith. Jake handed him the statement he had already taken from Smith. Smith followed Matt into the office and took a seat while Matt read the statement Jake had taken.

Unlike Joe Henderson, Lewis Smith seemed unfazed by the commotion surrounding the murders at the museum. His large square frame sat comfortably in its middle-aged muscles and fat with not a whisper of self-consciousness or fear. He had a shrewd look about the eyes as if he had seen it all before, and anything you told him now was bound to be anti-climactic.

"It says here that you didn't see or hear anything unusual in the museum last night, Mr. Smith."

"Yes, that's right. Everything was perfectly normal. I made my rounds the same as I do every night; and I didn't notice anything wrong."

"How many times do you walk through the museum?"

"Well, my job is to make sure all the entrances and exits are secure at night. It takes from 45 minutes to an hour to walk through the whole museum, depending on the route I take. I usually make about five rounds a night."

"Describe where your rounds took you last night."

Lewis gave Matt a precise verbal layout of where he walked through the museum. The landmarks didn't mean much to Matt, but he was pleased with the level of detail.

"How many times did you stop to talk to Joe Henderson?"

"I had to wake him up a couple of times as I went past the security console right after he came on duty. He was snoring loud enough to rouse the dead. I guess he slept it off, because he was wide awake during the last rounds I made. We talk for 10 or 15 minutes sometimes. That's how I take my breaks. It's lonely in here at night, and we're glad for each other's company."

"Do you make your rounds at certain times?"

"Not really. I walk through every couple of hours, but I don't do it on a schedule."

"Did you see anyone at all in the museum during third-shift?"

"No, there wasn't a soul in here but Joe and me."

"Are you absolutely certain nobody was in here?"

"I'm positive, lieutenant. The staff don't usually work third-shift unless there's a major exhibit that's behind schedule. That's the only time they burn the midnight oil around here."

"Could someone have stayed late, forgot to sign in, and left without being noticed?"

"That's a possibility, especially with Joe sleeping the way he was last night."

"Do all of the outside doors have computerized locks?"

"No. Just the main entrances off the Mall and Constitution Avenue. But the rest of the doors have damned good locks. We've never had a break-in in the 25 years I've been working here."

"Did you notice whether there was a sign-in log at the security console last night?"

"No, I didn't notice, but there usually is."

"What time did you leave this morning?"

"I clocked out at 10 past eight, the same time I leave every morning."

"Did you see Colonel Kendricks or Willis Brandt after you clocked out this morning?"

"I don't think I'm supposed to tell you this, but Chief Brandt came over to my house to ask me about what happened last night."

"What'd you tell him?"

"The same thing I told you, lieutenant. The truth."

"That's all for now, Mr. Smith. I'll probably have some follow-up questions later on."

"Who killed those men?"

"That's a good question, Mr. Smith. I hoped you could

tell me."

"I don't know anything about those murders."

"No one else does, either, Mr. Smith. But that's what makes my job interesting. I'll find out what happened last night. And I guarantee you it won't be a pretty sight. All this high-toned culture can't hide the stink of two brutal murders," Matt insisted as he went over to the door and motioned for the next security guard to come in.

Lewis Smith's unflappable composure faltered briefly as he gave Matt an anxious glance before leaving the office. The remaining security guards came into the room one by one. As a group, they had stopped complaining about seven o'clock, having been lulled into stupefaction by the interminable waiting with nothing to do. Some had tried shooting the breeze, but it got stale quickly, since all of them wanted to be at home rather than where they were. Matt questioned them with the same attention to detail he had given Earl Simms, Joe Henderson, and Lewis Smith, but with far less promising results. It was nearly midnight when he finished. Jake staggered into Dr. Fisher's office and collapsed into a chair.

"Man, if you don't let me out of here, I'll go stir crazy. All those damn guards, and I still don't now what the hell happened. Did you learn anything more?"

"Nothing about the homicides. They're playing us, partner."

"How so?"

"Don't know for certain, but they're playing us real cheap. Kendricks and Brandt got to Lewis Smith and Joe

Henderson before we did."

"You think they told them to lie about what happened?"

"Maybe. They all know a hell of a lot more than they're telling us. But we still have a lot of ground to cover. We haven't questioned the maintenance people or the professional staff yet. I've still got Kendricks and Brandt to go, too."

"Not tonight, Matt. I've had it."

"Same here, partner."

Matt and Jake found Chief Brandt at the security console with the second-shift guard, Wilbur Daniels.

"Col. Kendricks told me to give this to you," Brandt said. It's the protocol Secretary Marshall set up for handling the emerald necklace. Col. Kendricks says you can examine the necklace whenever you want to, but it has to stay here at the Smithsonian."

"Where is it now?"

"I don't know for certain, but it's under tight security wherever it is."

"Did our forensics specialist finish his examination?"

"Sure thing. Your man's been gone for hours, lieutenant."

"I guess somebody got what they came for," Matt concluded as he and Jake walked toward the employee entrance. "I want to talk to you and Col. Kendricks first thing in the morning, Brandt. What time do you get here?" he called back over his shoulder.

"Eight o'clock. I have staff meeting at eight-thirty."

"I'll see you in your office at eight."

"Col. Kendricks' office is in the Castle."

"Yeah, right," Matt called without looking back.

"Good riddance!" Brandt exclaimed. "I thought we'd never get rid of them."

"Here's the second-shift sign-in log from last night, chief. I already gave a copy to Lieutenant Alexander. There were only five staff people here during the second-shift."

"You know better than that, Wilbur. The professional staff sign in whenever they please. Some of them have never signed in once, even though they work late all the time. They think our security system is a joke. Col. Kendricks has complained all the way up to Secretary Marshall, but it doesn't do a damned bit of good. We can't enforce the policy."

"Sometimes even the ones that sign in don't bother to sign out," Wilbur Daniels agreed.

"The professional staff won't follow our security procedures; but whenever anything goes wrong, they always blame security. It's always our fault. They'll blame us for the murders, too; and we don't even know which staff members were in the museum last night," Brandt complained as he got ready to leave.

"Looks like you worked two shifts today, chief. It's almost 12 o'clock."

"Don't remind me, Wilbur."

Matt and Jake arrived at Fourth District Headquarters at twelve-thirty. Jake dropped Matt off and went home. Matt went to the Homicide Division's Forensics Laboratory in the basement. Sam Johnson was preparing to leave as Matt walked through the double doors of the lab.

"I knew you'd show up before I could get out of here, Alexander."

"I'm glad to see you too, Sam. So what's the deal with the necklaces?"

"Both necklaces were clean. No blood, no prints, no fibers, nothing; too clean, if you ask me. Somebody got to them before we did."

"Kendricks and his staff are trying to play us, man. You got anything else interesting?" Matt asked, looking around the lab.

"I haven't had time to do any tests yet, Alexander. We spent most of the time getting the blood swatches ready."

"You find anything left by the shooter?"

"Can't tell yet. I've been trying to imagine how two stiffs get shot up in a relatively open space without leaving any evidence that they tried to fight their way out of there."

"Yeah, I know what you mean. There should have been evidence of a struggle."

"I did find several shoe prints in all that dust in there, but they were faint, and they didn't have any blood on them. I took impressions of Kendrick's and Simm's shoes. I got some good shots of the blood spatter evidence, and that ought to tell us something; but I'm going back down there tomorrow morning to take another good look around."

"What time are you going? I'll meet you there."

"Around seven."

"Jesus, Sam. Gimme a break and make it later."

"Seven-thirty and not a minute later, Alexander. I have a lot of testing to do tomorrow."

Matt and Sam talked for several minutes more in the

Matt and Sam talked for several minutes more in the parking lot. When he got home, Matt found both children asleep in bed with his wife Carla, and the television still going full blast. He took his four-year old daughter, Jennifer, to her bedroom first. His two-year old son Robert woke up as Matt placed him in his crib. His screams followed Matt back to his bedroom.

"Good grief! What's the baby screaming for now, honey?"

"I put him in his crib. Why do you keep letting the baby sleep with you, Carla? He's got to learn to sleep in his own bed."

"I'd rather let him sleep with me than listen to him screaming his lungs out every night," Carla insisted, dragging herself out of bed to comfort her screaming son.

"Let him scream, Carla. It won't hurt him. He's using all that noise to control you, just like Pavlov's dog."

"If I weren't so sleepy, I'd let you have it for calling me a dog, Matthew Alexander."

Matt laughed. "It's just a figure of speech, baby. You know Pavlov's dog was conditioned to salivate every time he heard a bell. You jump up and put Robbie in the bed with us every time he screams out at night. He's got your number."

"You don't have to tell me about Pavlov's dog. I'm the psychologist in this family, and I can't stand all that racket when I'm trying to get some sleep."

"He knows you can't stand it. That's why he wakes up every night screaming like clockwork. When are you going to get wise, Carla? Let him scream himself to sleep a couple of times, and all this madness will be over." Matt closed their bedroom door to drown out the screams.

Carla got up to turn on the intercom in their bedroom.

"Don't touch that intercom!" Matt insisted, blocking Carla's path. "Let him scream."

Carla got back into bed as Jenny entered their bedroom.

"Daddy, make Robbie be quiet. I can't go to sleep."

"Nobody can stand that racket, Matthew. How are we supposed to get any sleep around here?"

Carla turned over in bed and put the pillow over her head to muffle the sound of her son's screams.

"Close the door to your room, Jenny. He'll stop after he tires himself out."

"I still hear him with my door closed, Daddy."

"Well, just pretend you can't hear him, honey. That way he'll think everybody else is asleep and he'll go to sleep, too," Matt said as he picked Jenny up and took her back to her room.

"Will you read me a story, Daddy? I always go to sleep when you read me a story."

"Okay, but only if you promise to be sound asleep when I finish the story."

"I promise, Daddy."

When Matt got back to his bedroom, he found Carla and Robbie in bed together, his son sucking from a bottle of warm milk with a very satisfied look in very wide awake eyes. Carla pretended to be asleep.

"This is a darned shame, Carla! You're letting him

for it. Didn't you tell me you had thrown that bottle away? I thought psychologists were supposed to know how to raise children."

"I'm not a child psychologist; and I do know how to raise my own son."

"By spoiling him rotten?"

"A little spoiling is good for a baby. They feel more secure if they know you love them," Carla insisted as she cradled her son close to her while he made noisy sucking sounds with his bottle.

"You have to love him enough to do what's best for him, not let him lead you around by the nose," Matt countered as he scooped his son from his wife's arms and carried him back to his crib where the screaming soon commenced again.

Matt returned to his bedroom and closed the door before undressing in their walk-in closet. Carla stretched and yawned as she channel surfed for a good movie. She asked Matt to bring her a glass of wine from the kitchen. The baby's screaming trailed off as Matt rummaged through the refrigerator. He eventually returned with a sandwich and a beer for himself and a glass of Zinfandel for her. He sat down in the chair next to the bed and ate his sandwich while Carla watched the movie "Devil In a Blue Dress " on television and talked to him at the same time.

"Why so late? Another murder?"

"Two homicides, at the Smithsonian, no less."

"At the Smithsonian? Who got killed?" she asked in surprise.

surprise.

"Two black men were shot in the Museum of Natural History."

"Who killed them?"

"Don't know, yet. It's a weird case; and the Smithsonian people haven't rolled out the red carpet for us, either."

"What's so strange about it? Black men are killed everyday in the District."

"They were dressed like African warriors ready for battle."

"That is weird. Why were they dressed like that?"

"I don't know, Carla."

"Two young black men dressed like African warriors killed in the Museum of Natural History. That's bizarre, Matthew."

"They were shot in an exhibit on Africa."

"Maybe they were Africans, honey. They could have been trying to take their cultural artifacts back. You know how European imperialist nations looted the cultural artifacts of undeveloped countries they were supposedly civilizing in the nineteenth century. They just took the treasures of countries like Greece and Egypt. They said they were doing it to save the artifacts from native thieves and plunderers, but why keep them now that those countries have stable governments and their own cultural institutions to preserve their history? I'm sure the Smithsonian has looted cultural treasures from a lot of African countries in its collection."

Matt listened intently as Carla talked.

Museum's gem collection."

"It was probably stolen from an African tribe, Matthew. The Africans who were murdered were just taking back what belonged to them in the first place."

Matt looked unconvinced.

"The Smithsonian's jewelry curator said the necklace probably came from Colombia, Central America, Carla."

"Even if the necklace didn't come from Africa, the emeralds probably did, just like the other natural resources that were plundered and stolen by those racist colonizing nations."

Matt yawned over the remnants of his sandwich and beer.

"Even if the necklace did originally belong to them, which I seriously doubt, they had no business breaking into the Museum of Natural History to steal it back."

"Look at Greece. They've done everything but crawl on their hands and knees to get the Elgin Marbles back; and the Oba of Benin has literally begged for the return of the Benin bronzes. Nineteenth century economic imperialists have become twentieth century cultural imperialists. They know that most of the treasures in their national museums were either looted or stolen, but what do they care? I don't see anything wrong with stealing back what was stolen from you in the first place."

"It's not worth dying for, Carla. What good did it do them? That emerald necklace is still in the Smithsonian's gem collection."

"Well, at least they tried to reclaim their cultural heritage," Carla insisted as she yawned and switched off the lamp on her nightstand. "Aren't you coming to bed, honey?"

"Not yet. I have some video tapes I need to look at before I go back to the Smithsonian tomorrow."

"All work and no play makes Matthew a very dull boy," Carla said drowsily as she sank deeper into her pillow and drifted off to sleep.

CHAPTER 5

When William Fisher, Wallace Kendricks, and Willis Brandt arrived at Andrew Marshall's office early the next day, they found the secretary deep into Kendricks' security report on the homicides. He read intently as he took slow sips from his coffee. When he finished the report, he looked worriedly around the room.

"Have you read this report, Bill?"

"I read it before I came over, Andy."

"You actually saw the victims on the security tapes, Wally?"

"Yes sir. Plain as the nose on your face. At least three cameras caught them going up the main staircase at 12:55 Wednesday morning. Both Joe Henderson and Lewis Smith were on duty, but they swear they didn't see or hear anybody in the museum around that time. Henderson was manning the security console so he should have seen them; but I'm certain he was sleep. It wouldn't be the first time."

"What do we pay your people for if they can't keep intruders from walking up the main staircase of the museum and stealing a priceless necklace?" Fisher asked.

Kendricks ignored Fisher's remark, directing his comments to Secretary Marshall.

"Natural History is a huge place, Mr. Secretary. There's no way we can police a museum that size with two men. I told you during our budget briefings that cutting my staff would compromise security. Nobody listened."

"Were the guards at their stations, Wally?"

"Lewis Smith was doing his job. He's the best man I have, sir; and Joe Henderson is the worst. Henderson is a drunk who comes to work smelling like a still. I have to pay Wilbur Daniels overtime to stay at the security console until Henderson shows up, because he's chronically late. I started termination proceedings on Henderson twice, and each time Fisher here stepped in and saved Henderson's job."

Secretary Marshall gave Fisher a hard stare.

"Joe Henderson has 25 in the civil service, Andy. We can't fire him just because he's having emotional problems over the death of his wife."

"Joe Henderson was a falling down drunk before his wife died, Fisher. What was your excuse for fighting to keep him when I tried to fire him three years ago?" Kendricks demanded.

"He got counseling from both AA and our EAP program, Andy. He stayed off the sauce until his wife died eight months ago."

"Joe Henderson is a marginal employee at best, and he's a serious risk to the museum's security. We should have gotten rid of him years ago," Kendricks insisted.

"There's no use in crying over spilt milk now, Wally. Do you have any idea how those men got into the museum?"

"When Brandt and I checked the entrances and exits early Wednesday morning, there was absolutely no sign of a break-in. All of the doors and windows on the ground level are wired into the alarm system. The alarm didn't go off Tuesday night or Wednesday morning. The power didn't go down, either. I don't know how they got in, sir."

"Joe Henderson was manning the staff entrance on the third-shift, Mr. Secretary. He says he didn't let anyone into the museum after midnight," Brandt added.

"Could they have gotten in during the second-shift?" the secretary asked.

"Wilbur Daniels had to let them in if they did. He swears his sign-in log is complete; and the only people who came in or left the museum after closing hours are on the second-shift sign-in log," Kendricks explained.

"Was there anything else unusual on the security tapes, Wally?"

"No, sir. We went over them quickly, but the only thing that stood out was the two men creeping up the stairs about one o'clock Wednesday morning. After that, they don't show up on the tapes."

"What about the museum staff? Were any staff people working the third-shift in Natural History Tuesday night?"

"Well, sir. There's no third-shift sign-in log, so there's no record of who was in the museum. Joe Henderson claims he didn't let anyone into the museum; but he can't be trusted."

"It's pretty common for staff working overtime not to sign the logs, Mr. Secretary," Brandt offered.

"That's right, sir," Kendricks agreed. "Our policy is for all staff to log in and out if they're in the museum after hours, but the policy is routinely ignored. Fact of the matter is, we don't know who was in the museum during third-shift Tuesday night."

"Christ! Do we know anything for certain?"

"Not much, Mr. Secretary."

"Are you sure the murdered men didn't work for us, Wally? I need to know if they've ever been employed anywhere at the Smithsonian."

"I've already checked with all the heads of departments at Natural History, and nobody recognized them. But that's not to say they never worked for us. I would need their social security numbers or fingerprints to make sure."

Andrew Marshall's secretary entered the office and informed him that several newspaper reporters and a television news crew were waiting in the reception area. The secretary grimaced.

"What should I tell them, Mr. Secretary?" she asked.

"Let them wait, dammit! Who needs this kind of negative exposure during congressional budget hearings?"

"Do you want me to get rid of them?" Kendricks asked.

"What's the use? They'll just come back until they

get their story."

"Did you finish the press release, Bill?"

"It's right here, Andy. I've included the few facts we know about the murders, and I referred them to the District Police for the rest."

The secretary passed a copy of the press release to Kendricks, who frowned as he read it.

"Is it absolutely necessary to tell them all this, Mr. Secretary?"

"I don't want the press to get the impression we're stonewalling them, Wally. If they think we're cooperating, they may cut us some slack. God only knows what the fallout will be on the Hill, though. Once the budget committee gets wind of the murders, we're in for a rough ride. They hate us up there since the *Enola Gay*."

"What should I tell the reporters?" Marshall's secretary asked again.

"Tell them I've scheduled a press conference for two o'clock this afternoon in my conference room. It's bad enough to have to put up with their crap at all; but I'm damned if I do it on their time. Tell them to come back at two."

Matt and Jake arrived at the museum at the same time as the eight o'clock meeting ended in Andrew Marshall's office. They were met by Captain Henry Bryant and a half-dozen uniformed officers waiting inside the staff entrance on Constitution Avenue.

"The commander wants a meeting in his office at one, Alexander."

"Why do I have to be there, Bryant? You've been do-

"Why do I have to be there, Bryant? You've been doing a first-rate job of keeping him informed behind my back."

"I don't know how to take that, lieutenant," Bryant replied, embarrassed by the snickers and smiles from his men.

"Take it anyway you please, Captain," Matt answered as he led the officers upstairs to the crime scene with Bryant breathing down his neck.

"I outrank you lieutenant; and if it wasn't for the fact that I'm retiring soon I'd have nailed your smart-assed mouth to the wall a long time ago."

Without breaking his stride, Matt turned to Bryant, gave him a deadly smile, and said, "I'm not buying any of your woof tickets today, man. If you want to get it on, just say the word and we'll see who gets nailed to the wall."

"Have mercy!" Jake howled with laughter. "You've just been invited to a whipping, partner, and I do believe you're the main course. Jake continued to laugh while Bryant slunk back among his own men.

"The Captain is sho-nuff feeling feisty today, man. Offering to whip you. That's one for the record books," Jake guffawed as he looked back at a humbled Captain Bryant.

"Can it, Jake. There's no point in rubbing his face in it."

When they arrived at the crime scene, they found Sam and his criminalists already on the job. Lois and Ruby waited for instructions from Sam as he sifted through the crime scene for the remnants of any evidence they might

Sam was down on his hands and knees.

Without looking up, Sam said, "You're late, lieutenant. It's nine o'clock."

"Give me a break, Sam. Found anything interesting this morning?"

"Not to speak of."

"Need any help?"

Sam stopped what he was doing long enough to look around at the six uniformed officers accompanying Captain Bryant.

"You call those clowns help? There's no way in hell I'd have them stomping through my crime scene."

"Suit yourself, Sam. I'll put them on the weapon search. Have you talked to the deputy medical examiner yet?"

"The autopsies are scheduled for this afternoon. I ought to have the slugs sometime today."

"We still don't have a weapon."

"You aren't going to find one, either. Whoever shot those bums hauled his ass out of this crime scene, quick. Not much trace of a killer left in here."

"Tell me something good, Sam."

Wallace Kendricks walked over to where Matt and Sam were talking. Chief Brandt followed his boss.

"You're just the man I want to see, lieutenant. I just left a meeting with the secretary, and he's scheduled a press conference for two o'clock this afternoon. He needs to meet with you before the press conference so you can bring him up to date on the murders."

"It's interesting you should bring that up, Kendricks.

We were just having a discussion about what a half-assed job you people are doing keeping us informed. Last night I found out you had the crust to interrogate the third-shift guards before we got to them. I warned you about obstruction of justice, but it's obvious you didn't take me seriously."

"I don't know what you're implying, lieutenant."

"The hell you don't know," Matt replied as he walked over to give the rest of the officers instructions on searching the museum for the murder weapon. Captain Bryant and his men followed Chief Brandt through the museum.

Matt, Jake, and Kendricks went down to the first floor office where Matt had been interrogating museum staff.

"About those video tapes, Kendricks, I . . ."

"We gave you all the third-shift tapes yesterday, man. What more do you want?"

"I already looked at those tapes. Both of the murder victims can be seen walking up the main stairs of the museum, but I'm sure you know that already."

"How would I know that? We gave you the only copy of the tapes we have."

"Let's can the bullshit, Kendricks; you know damned well you made copies of those tapes. You told me you only run 10 cameras during third-shift, but why should I believe you? For all I know, you had all the damned cameras running all night."

"You're barking up the wrong tree, lieutenant. Check with our videographer and you'll see that we only run 10 cameras on third-shift."

"That's just the problem, Kendricks. He's the Smithsonian's videographer, and it's the Smithsonian's video library. Who's to say you haven't gotten rid of the extra tapes by now? Both you and Brandt have been checking my shit tighter than white on rice. I know about your visits to Henderson and Smith yesterday. But just for the record, Kendricks, if I find out that either one of you is playing fast and loose with the evidence in this case, I'll take you down so fast you won't see it coming. That's a promise from me to you."

On his way out of the office, Kendricks did a slow burn as he passed Martha Darden, the first professional staff member to be interrogated. When she entered the office, Matt looked down at the list on the desk in front of him.

"I take it you're Martha Darden."

"Yes, that's right."

"I'm Lieutenant Matthew Alexander, Miss Darden. According to the museum's sign-in log for the evening of Tuesday, June sixth, you left the museum at 10 o'clock the evening of the murders."

"Yes, that's right."

"Did you know that two men were killed in the museum later that same night?"

"Everybody knows it, lieutenant."

"What's your job at the museum, Miss Darden?"

"I'm Assistant Curator for the Native American collection in the Division of Anthropology."

"Do you often work late?"

"Yes, I do. I'm not married, so I don't have a family to

go home to. People in my division think I'm stupid to put in the amount of overtime I do, but I'd rather work than watch that nonsense they put on television. They stopped paying me overtime years ago, but I get compensatory time, which is just as good for vacations and time off."

"Why did you stay late on Tuesday night?"

"We're getting ready for a major exhibit on the Plains Indians; and I'm responsible for researching the exhibition script. I've got a lot of work to finish before the end of the year, so I stay late most nights."

"Where were you working Tuesday night?"

"In my office."

"Was anyone working with you?"

"The senior curator, George Bayless, was here. He's swamped with work, too, but he left before I did."

"Did you see any other staff working late Tuesday night?"

"There was someone else on the third floor. Whoever it was standing in the shadows near the central staircase when I was coming out of the ladies room, but I couldn't tell who it was."

"Are you certain you saw someone up there last night?"

"Absolutely. I'm very careful about who's here at night, especially in my area. As a matter of fact, I usually call a security guard to escort me through the museum when I leave. Several years ago, a staff member was raped out in the parking lot. I've been very careful since then."

"Could you tell whether the person you saw was a man or a woman?"

"I'm almost certain it was a man, but I wouldn't swear

to it. I didn't see him very clearly before he walked away."

"Where did he go?"

"He walked in the direction of the service elevators. I suppose it could have been one of the maintenance people, but I don't think so. He didn't have a cleaning cart."

Matt passed Martha Darden his copy of the sign-in log from the previous night.

"Could the person you saw be one of the people on this list?"

"Maybe, but I can't say for certain."

"Did you hear anything unusual while you were in your office?"

"No, I didn't. I left at 10 o'clock, and up to then everything seemed perfectly normal."

"So the only other staff person you knew was working late was the senior curator for your division?"

"Yes, that's right."

"That's all for now, Miss Darden."

"Do you have any idea who killed those men?"

"We're getting there," Matt indicated as he escorted Martha Darden to the door where he found George Bayless, the senior curator of the Native American Division, waiting his turn to be questioned. George Bayless held his slight frame ramrod straight as he perched on the edge of his chair. His appearance was *de rigueur*—complete with bow tie, wire-rimmed spectacles, blue blazer, tan slacks, and penny loafers. Bayless was younger than Martha Darden by about 10 years; and he regularly pushed a shock of thick brown hair from his right eye as he regarded Matt coolly. He did not speak until he was spoken to.

"What do you do at the museum, Mr. Bayless?"

"I'm Curator of the Native American Collection in the Anthropology Division."

"How long have you been in that position?"

"For the past five years. Before that I was a professor of Cultural Anthropology at Dartmouth College."

"How long has Martha Darden worked for you?"

"Martha was with the division when I took over. She was hired by my predecessor and was very loyal to him. Most of the staff were, for that matter."

"How many staff people do you manage?"

"Fifteen positions report to me, but two are vacant."

"How many staff worked late this past Tuesday night?"

"Just Martha and myself from my division. Martha stays late practically every night. I've been doing it a lot myself since we started developing the new exhibit on the Plains Indians. I have a lot of work to keep on schedule."

"What time did you leave Tuesday?"

"Around eight."

"Could a staff member sign out and stay in the museum?"

"I suppose they could; but why would anyone want to do that?"

"Why would anyone want to murder two men?" Matt asked, not expecting an answer. "Did you see any other staff members in the museum while you here last night?"

"Well, yes, I did. Besides Martha, there was an assistant curator who left when I did and two people from zoology."

"Do you know their names?"

George Bayless mentioned three people, all of whom had signed out on the log.

"Are you certain there was no one else in the museum?"

"No, I'm not certain. It's not unusual for staff to work late and forget to sign the log, so someone else might easily have been in here."

"Do you have any idea why those men were killed Tuesday night, Mr. Bayless?"

George Bayless looked both surprised and cautious when he heard the question.

"I thought it was facts you were interested in, Lieutenant Alexander, not opinions."

"Facts are important, but so are opinions . . . from intelligent people."

George Bayless wasn't flattered. He gave Matt a hard, calculating look before answering, "The murders are absolutely appalling. We have not had a murder at one of our museums since I've been working here, and we've certainly never had one where the murder victims were dressed in costume. Frankly, lieutenant, I'm at a total loss to understand why they were dressed like that, who they are, or why they were killed. It's created a very bad situation for us right in the middle of our congressional budget hearings."

"The murder of two men ought to have a higher priority than your budget hearings, Mr. Bayless."

"The killings are unfortunate, of course, especially for the dead men, but this will negatively impact our budget hearings. There's no doubt about that."

"That's all for now, Mr. Bayless. Thanks for your cooperation."

George Bayless quickly exited the office. Matt followed him out to refill his coffee mug. Jake was at the coffee machine, too, taking a breather between security guards.

"How's it going, partner?" Jake asked.

"Not good, man."

"The security guards were a bust, too. I've just about finished with them. Who do you want me to talk to next?"

"The support staff. I'm going to give the maintenance people to Bryant. That ought to make him feel real important."

"There's a call for you, lieutenant," Willis Brandt's elderly female secretary told Matt. "It's Secretary Marshall's office."

Matt took the call and spent the next few minutes negotiating a mutually agreeable time to meet with the secretary. The rest of the morning passed uneventfully in that Matt learned nothing from the remaining staffers that he hadn't already known; and Jake learned nothing new at all from the last of the first-shift security guards. At one o'clock, Matt left for his meeting with Secretary Marshall.

When Matt arrived at Andrew Marshall's conference room in the Castle, he found that Fisher, Willis Brandt, Wallace Kendricks, and Bernard Wampler, Director of the Hirshorn Museum, had arrived before him. Marshall's assistant was also there, taking notes. Marshall was sitting at the head of his rectangular conference table. Matt sat directly opposite him at the other end of the table.

"I see you finally decided to honor us with your presence, Lieutenant Alexander," the secretary derisively commented.

"I don't have much time, Secretary Marshall. Since you asked for the meeting, can we get to the point?"

"As I said earlier, lieutenant, I've rescheduled my press conference from two to three. I asked for this meeting so you can bring me up to date on what you've learned about the murders so far."

"I can't tell what we've found out about the homicides so you can turn around and tell it to the press. It's a violation of departmental policy to brief anyone outside the department on the status of ongoing investigations. Besides that, I'm trying to find out who killed those men, and I'm not about to sabotage my own investigation by putting the facts about this case on the street."

Secretary Marshall bristled at Matt's patronizing tone. The other men around the table maintained their silence as the tension escalated.

"You miss my point entirely, Lieutenant. I don't want to know the minute details of the investigation. I simply need to understand the chronology of what happened in the Museum of Natural History."

"You miss my point, Mr. Secretary. When you're up to your neck in a homicide investigation, you can learn a lot from your suspects if the particulars of the crime haven't already been broadcast all over creation. That's a lot from your suspects if the particulars of the crime haven't already been broadcast all over creation. That's why we keep our evidence close to the vest."

"Everybody at the Smithsonian knows those two men were shot to death, Lieutenant Alexander. Are you telling me that I can't say they were shot in my press conference?"

"I wish you wouldn't, Mr. Secretary. The slower the facts about this case become public knowledge, the better chance we have to find the shooter."

"Dammit, Lieutenant Alexander! There's no point in calling a press conference, if I can't say anything about the crime. You've got to cut me some slack on this. The media is swarming all over us."

"Here's a press release I wrote for the secretary, lieutenant," Fisher said as he passed one sheet of double-spaced type to Matt. "Andy thinks we need to flesh it out more, so the press won't think we're holding out on them."

"The press isn't my problem," Matt replied.

"It sure the hell is a problem for the Smithsonian," the secretary swore. "We don't need them breathing down our necks right now. We're still trying to get through our budget hearings, and how this thing plays out in the press could kill us on the Hill. I want the media to leave the press conference satisfied that I've been open with them about the murders."

"That's not my problem, Mr. Secretary; but I'll go to your press conference and tell the press to piss off myself."

of all now."

"My advice is to let the District Police handle the media, Mr. Marshall. This press release states facts that shouldn't be released to the public, like how the victims were dressed. If the media wants to know the particulars, refer them to the Homicide Division or to me."

"You refuse to understand the position we're in, lieutenant. We have to meet with the press and discuss the murders. We don't have a choice," Fisher insisted. Matt rose to leave.

"I guess that's one way to look at it, Fisher. I can't help you on this one, but I strongly advise you not to distribute that press release."

Secretary Marshall was livid as Matt walked toward the door.

"Tell him what we've decided about the necklace" he said to Bernard Wampler.

Wampler looked caught in the middle as he cleared his throat and turned to Matt.

"We've decided that we can't give the emerald necklace adequate protection in the secretary's office, lieutenant. So we're going to keep it in the vault over in the Museum of Natural History along with the rest of the gem collection."

"So you refuse to provide a chain of custody for the necklace?" Matt asked Marshall.

"We can't protect the necklace over here, lieutenant. I've checked with the mayor and Chief Carter, and they both approved putting the genuine necklace back into the vault for security reasons," Secretary Marshall replied with a satisfied look on his face. Matt knew when he had been beaten, so he left the conference room and closed the door behind him.

"What about the press conference, Mr. Secretary?" asked Kendricks.

"It's still on."

"And the press release?"

"That, too," the secretary replied as he walked back to his office.

"Looks like the shit's getting ready to hit the fan," Kendricks said to the other men around the conference table after Matt left.

After the meeting, Matt returned to the museum in an angry mood. He found Captain Bryant ensconced in an administrative office on the lower level. Bryant had a uniformed officer taking notes while he questioned security guards. Matt returned to his temporary office on the same level and called Steve Mitchell to get an update on the autopsies. The deputy medical examiner told him the first one was scheduled for three o'clock that afternoon. Steve informed Matt that Sam Johnson had already been to the morgue and had taken a full set of fingerprints from both victims.

Matt ate the cold lunch Jake had left for him before resuming interviewing staff. He then questioned museum employees for four hours until he was interrupted by a call from Commander Lloyd Cullison shortly after five o'clock. Cullison informed him that coverage of Secretary Marshall's three o'clock press conference had been on all the local television stations. He also told Matt to meet him in Chief of Police Jefferson Carter's office as soon as possible in order to brief the chief for a seven o'clock press conference.

Matt was seething as he drove back to the Museum of Natural History after Chief Carter's press conference. The chief had tried to be as noncommittal as possible, but the press had been on a feeding frenzy. During the press conference, Chief Carter had referred all questions about the victims and the circumstances surrounding their deaths to Matt. Since Secretary Marshall had already distributed the press release to the media at his earlier news conference, Matt had had very little wiggle room when asked about the specifics of the case by reporters.

He had to confirm the fact that the District Police didn't know the victims' identities. In his press conference, Secretary Marshall had made a point of informing the media that the victims had never worked for the Smithsonian and no identification had been found on their bodies when they were found. Matt could see his investigation being sabotaged before his eyes. Too much information had hit the streets before he had time to make sense of the few facts they had uncovered so far. The case had started to run away from him, and he would have to struggle hard to stay on top of the investigation. It was a very bad situation all around.

Matt returned to the museum at seven-thirty p.m. He noted that Captain Bryant was nowhere to be seen. Matt and Jake finished questioning the second-shift security guards, none of whom admitted seeing or hearing anything connected with the homicides before the midnight shift change, so Matt had learned no more at the end of the day than he had known that morning.

The two detectives left the museum at 10 o'clock that evening. Matt went back to headquarters, where he stopped in at the Crime Lab to talk to Sam before going up to his own office. Sam showed Matt the evidence Steve Mitchell had sent over from the medical examiner's office, including the preliminary autopsy reports, the bullets, and the costumes the victims were wearing. Sam informed Matt that he had already begun to search the AFIS data base with the victims' fingerprints, but he warned Matt not to be overly optimistic about a match, putting even more of a damper on his already low spirits.

At home Thursday night, after he sorted through everything he had read or gathered about the investigation, Matt concluded that he had made scant progress in identifying the victims, finding the murder weapon, figuring out a motive for the murder, or identifying the shooter. He reluctantly conceded that his prospects for solving the case quickly were evaporating.

CHAPTER 6

A TV news crew was waiting for Matt when he arrived for work at eight o'clock that Friday morning. He grudgingly gave them 10 minutes before escaping to his office, where Jake was waiting for him.

"Our almighty commander has already called for you twice this morning, man. You better hotfoot it on down there before he comes to get you."

"Let him come. I'm not going anywhere until I drink my coffee," Matt insisted as he removed the lid from a large steaming cup.

Jake smiled, sat back in his chair, and waited to see whether the mountain would come to Mohammed.

"Secretary Marshall blew your case out of the water yesterday, man. Didn't you tell him not to give all that information out to the press when you met with him yesterday?"

"Yes, I told the asshole, but he did it anyway. He's trying to save the Smithsonian's bacon up on the Hill. Can you believe he had the nerve to ask me to brief him on my case? I guess if I had been dumb enough to tell him anything else, he would have blabbed that to the press, too. I owe him big time."

"Man, did you see the amount of coverage those homicides got on television last night? It was on all the channels."

"Don't remind me, Jake."

The telephone rang.

"For you, man. Cullison again."

Matt answered the telephone and listened as Lloyd Cullison dressed him down for being late for his meeting. Matt's face hardened as he listened to his commander's harangue. After he rang off, Matt continued drinking his coffee and scanning the *Washington Post*.

"Looks like Cullison's on the rampage this morning," Jake commented.

"So what else is new?" Matt replied as he got up and took several files from his desk before leaving for Cullison's first floor office.

When Matt entered Cullison's office, he found Sam Johnson and Captain Bryant already there. Cullison was irate, Matt was pissed, Bryant was still angry with Matt for dressing him down in front of his men, and Sam was intrigued by all the possibilities for a first-rate blow out.

"Sit down, Alexander," Cullison ordered.

Matt pulled a chair up in front of the desk next to Sam Johnson.

"The next time I schedule a meeting for eight o'clock, I want you in my office at eight, Hot Shot! But I guess it's hard to make eight o'clock meetings when you keep bankers' hours."

"I was here at eight o'clock, Lloyd. Reporters from

Channel 4 and the *Washington Post* were waiting for me downstairs. I was talking to them when you called my office the first time."

"I might buy that, Alexander, if you weren't always late for my meetings. I don't get any damned respect from you; and I've had it up to here with your attitude," Lloyd insisted as he made a slicing motion over his head with his right hand.

Sam Johnson was disappointed when Matt took his tongue lashing without a defense. Bryant couldn't disguise his pleasure at the way the meeting had begun.

"Have you found the shooter, Alexander?"

"No, Lloyd, I haven't."

"Have you found the weapon?"

"No, Lloyd, I haven't."

"Have you identified the victims?"

"No, Lloyd, I haven't."

"Didn't I put you in charge of this homicide investigation?"

"Yes, Lloyd, you did."

"So what the hell have you been doing for the past two days?"

"I haven't been sitting around on my ass watching my fingernails grow like some people in this division," Matt replied, looking in Captain Bryant's direction.

Sam perked up.

"Just what the hell is that supposed to mean?" Lloyd demanded.

"What's the point of this meeting, Lloyd? Do you want me to brief you on the investigation or not?"

Lloyd ignored Matt and asked Sam for his briefing first.

Sam's was quick and thorough. He discussed the preliminary post-mortem results, confirming that each of the victims had been killed by two .22-caliber bullets to the head and chest, all of which had been recovered by the Medical Examiner. Sam also discussed the blood stains, hair, fiber, and other trace evidence recovered from the crime scene, as well as the fingerprints taken from the victims. He said he hadn't found any prints or trace evidence on either necklace, a fact which Sam said was strange considering that the genuine emerald necklace had been found on the victim whose hands were covered in some type of gray powder which Sam hadn't identified yet. He concluded his briefing by indicating that few of his tests had been completed.

"Did you get the photographs I asked for Sam?" Matt asked.

"Yeah, here they are," Sam replied as he passed Matt an envelope containing eight-by-ten head shots of each of the victims.

Matt looked through the pictures one by one.

"What about the fingerprints, Johnson? Have you processed them through the AFIS yet?" Lloyd asked.

"I'm still matching their prints through the data base. I should know something soon."

"You said the necklace found on the victim was the real McCoy?"

Sam looked at Matt before answering, "Yeah, that's what they say, but you have to ask the lieutenant about that, commander."

Lloyd finally turned his attention to Matt.

"Sam said he found a stolen emerald necklace on one of the bodies. How did it get there?"

"The working assumption is that the victims broke into the museum and stole the necklace. But there was no sign of forced entry into the museum or the gem exhibit; and both the museum's security people and the company that installed the security system swear it wasn't breached Tuesday night. To get into the gem exhibit you have to know three separate codes held by three different people in addition to the combination to a first-rate locking mechanism at the back of the case. So if the system wasn't broken into, that means that three men, Wallace Kendricks, Willis Brandt, and Henry Hughes had to conspire to steal the necklace and kill the victims."

"That's ridiculous," Lloyd insisted. "Wallace Kendricks would never get involved in anything illegal."

"I don't know about Kendricks' honesty, Lloyd; but I agree that a conspiracy is unlikely, considering that the necklace was left at the scene. Anyway, after the genuine necklace was taken out of the display case, the homicide victims left a first-rate fake. If those guys hadn't been killed, I don't think the theft would have been noticed for months."

"You think two young men could have engineered all that, Alexander?"

"Doesn't seem likely to me."

"So what happened over there?"

"Your guess is as good as mine, Lloyd. But your good friend Colonel Kendricks has been doing a bang-up job of covering the Smithsonian's tracks."

"What do you mean? I thought he was cooperating with you."

"Oh, they've been very cooperative on the surface. The problem is that Kendricks and his security people are getting to the evidence in this investigation before we do, and by the time we get there, they've covered their tracks and made sure the Smithsonian comes up smelling like a rose. They're trying to control the damage on Capitol Hill."

"You're wrong about the colonel, Alexander," Bryant insisted. "He's helped us every step of the way."

"Do you have any proof of what you say, Alexander?" Lloyd asked.

"Kendricks and his security chief, Willis Brandt, left the museum for four hours on Wednesday, the day the bodies were discovered. We didn't know where the hell they went; and when they got back, they lied about where they had been. As it turns out, they left the museum to question the third-shift security guards before we could talk to them. I also have a suspicion that Kendricks and Brandt have doctored the video tapes that were running the night of the homicides. You can see the homicide victims creeping up the main staircase, but you don't see them coming down again.

"Besides that, nobody else at the Smithsonian admits knowing anything about the victims or the homicides. We have no way of knowing which staff members were in the museum the night of the murders because the sign-in log for the third-shift has conveniently disappeared. The two security guards on duty when the homicides occurred claim they didn't see or hear anything, even though the one manning the security console should have seen the murder victims on the monitors around one o'clock Wednesday morning. The list goes on and on, Lloyd."

"You still don't have a lead on who the stiffs are?"

"Not a whisper. If Sam can't match their prints, I'll have to run these pictures in the daily newspapers. I'm sending their pictures to all of the African embassies in town, too, to see if we can get a nibble in that direction."

"You think they're African?"

"They were dressed like it; but who knows?"

"Did you check to see if they came in a vehicle? They wouldn't have taken the bus or the subway dressed like that."

"Yeah, we checked that. There's no record of an unclaimed vehicle being towed from anywhere near the museum on Wednesday."

"This is the damnedest case, Alexander. You haven't nailed anything down; and the Smithsonian is making a full-court press on the downtown brass to get this case solved. Chief Carter is breathing down my neck to close this case, yesterday."

"The only thing the Smithsonian cares about is their goddamned budget hearing," Matt insisted.

"That's not the way I see it, Commander," Bryant countered. "I think they want to solve this case as much as we do."

"Have you finished interviewing all the museum employees yet? Lloyd asked Matt.

"Not yet. We're trying to finish that up today, if we can get Bryant to stay long enough to do some work. How many people did you question yesterday, Bryant?"

"I wasn't keeping count, Alexander; but I've pulled my weight on this case. That's for damned sure."

"Yeah, right, Bryant. I was born yesterday; but I stayed awake all night."

"I'd like a report from you by the end of the day, Alexander."

"Sure, but it won't include anymore than I've told you already, Lloyd."

"That's fine. I have to brief Chief Carter first thing tomorrow, and I want to give him a hard copy of the report."

Commander Cullison concluded the meeting at nine-thirty.

Matt gave the pictures of the victims to Jake when he returned to his office.

"Sam is still trying to match the victims' prints against the AFIS. If he doesn't score, we need to have these photographs ready to go ASAP. If I don't get these victims ID'd quick, this case is going up in smoke."

"Where you off to?"

"Howard University to talk to one of my old professors; but I'll meet you at the Smithsonian at one o'clock." Matt stopped at the crime lab where he found Sam in his office.

"You here again, Alexander?"

"Have you processed the victims' clothing yet?"

"I wouldn't go so far as to call it clothing, but we have gone through one set."

"I need to borrow the items for a couple of hours, Sam. I want to show them to an expert on African culture to see what he makes of them."

Sam gave Matt a warning look.

"You know it's against my policy to let evidence out of my custody until the trial, Alexander."

"Yeah, I know how hard-nosed you are, Sam."

"Hard-nosed, my ass. It'll be my neck in the noose, if my evidence comes up missing."

"I promise to guard those clothes with my life, Sam."

"If you fuck with my evidence, I'll kill you myself," Sam threatened as he went back into the forensics laboratory's evidence room and removed two oversized clear plastic bags.

"Thanks, Sam. I owe you one."

Matt entered the administrative offices of Howard University's History Department shortly after 10 o'clock. He told the older of two secretaries that he had an appointment with Dr. Anthony Phelps before taking a seat outside Dr. Phelps' office. Ten minutes later, Dr. Phelps ushered an elderly female faculty member from his office into the corridor, giving her positive assurances about her concerns along the way. He closed the door to the History Department after her and breathed a huge sigh of relief.

"Gloria, don't ever let Dr. Hazleton in to see me before I've had my morning coffee. I can't stand the strain," he laughed as he walked over to Matt and shook his hand.

"Mr. Alexander. It's good to see a prized pupil, even if he is the one who got away."

"Don't write me off completely, Dr. Phelps. I may turn up on your doorstep yet."

"No, you won't. You're one of the few students I taught during my 25 years at Howard University who knew exactly what he wanted and precisely where to go to get it. You won't come back here.

"Gloria, get two cups of coffee for us and don't disturb me for the next hour. What have you brought for me to see, Mr. Alexander?"

Matt was genuinely pleased to see his old professor. Over six feet tall, Dr. Anthony Phelps was still trim, disarming, and distinguished looking. And while he had grayed around the temples, his thick, wavy hair was still mostly black. Matt's first impression of Dr. Phelps 10 years before had been that he was too handsome to be intelligent. Matt had been wrong.

Matt placed the two plastic bags on top of Dr. Phelps' desk. Dr. Phelps removed the animal skin loincloth, the feathered headdress, the rattle, the armband, and the ankle bracelet.

"I guess you've heard about the murders at the Smithsonian by now, Dr. Phelps."

"Who hasn't, Mr. Alexander?" Dr. Phelps replied as he examined the costumes.

"One of the homicide victims was wearing this outfit. I wanted to see if you could tell me whether this stuff was authentic and where it came from in Africa."

"He was killed wearing this?"

"Yes, they were both dressed alike. We haven't been able to identify them, so we don't know whether they were Africans."

Dr. Phelps took the feathered headdress in his hands. He examined it for several minutes before walking over to his bookshelves and taking several large volumes down.

"I'm almost certain that headdress is Congolese. I've seen one like it before. It's just a question of locating the right text."

He leafed through several books simultaneously.

"Here it is. I knew I'd find it. It *is* Congolese. The headdress is typical of the Bakongo, an ethnic group from the Old Kingdom of the Congo who live between the Kwango and Kasai Rivers in Zaire. The Bakongo tribe lived across a vast territory in the old Congo, so when European nations laid the national boundaries of Angola, the Republic of the Congo which is now Zaire, and the Congo Republic, the Bakongo were split into three national groups, even though they are just one ethnic group.

"Look at this, Mr. Alexander," Dr. Phelps said, pointing to a large colored photograph in the book. "It's the same headdress, the same animal-skin loincloth, and the same shield. It's Bakongo, all right, no doubt about it."

"That narrows the number of embassies we'll have to talk to, Dr. Phelps."

"You said you haven't identified the murdered men yet?"

"That's right. From what you've told me, it seems there's a good possibility that they're African, which complicates things a lot."

"Did you see any ritual facial or body scars?"

"No, they didn't have any. They were just about naked, too, so not much was covered up."

"So there weren't any body scars?"

"No scars, but they were covered from head to foot in some type of thick yellow oil. Their bodies were so greasy, the men from the Medical Examiner's caught hell putting them in body bags."

"Grease. Umph . . . fascinating."

"Why would they grease themselves up like that?"

"Simple, really. The grease is a charm to ward off harm. Tribal warriors often painted or greased themselves with a special potion which had been blessed by the shaman, sorcerer, or witch doctor to keep evil away. Shows they practiced traditional African religion. This rattle is a strong indication that they were into voodoo. See these large teeth? They're probably from a lion, a sign of strength and power. My guess is that your victims are probably African."

"Is there any one particular group in Africa that oils themselves before battle?"

"It all depends on the cultural practice. Indigenous religions differ from culture to culture and from age to age, Mr. Alexander, but the practice of magic remains remarkably consistent across all cultures and is virtually the same now as it was four thousand years ago. Voodoo is nothing but African indigenous religion, remnants actually of the religion our slave ancestors brought to this country during the Middle Passage.

"Looks like their voodoo didn't save them."

"It never does; but that doesn't stop people from believing in their magic charms, spells, and potions."

"Maybe we shouldn't dismiss their voodoo so quickly, Dr. Phelps. They managed to steal a $10 million emerald necklace from the gem exhibit."

Dr. Phelps gasped in surprise.

"A $10 million emerald necklace! You're joking."

"I wish I was. It has emeralds the size of pigeon eggs. We recovered it from one of the victim's bodies."

"Fascinating combination, voodoo and a $10 million necklace."

"Do you know anything about the Bakongo people mining emeralds, Dr. Phelps?"

"No. I'm pretty sure they don't mine emeralds in Zaire. But emeralds are mined across the border from Zaire in the North of Zambia. Zambia is the second largest producer of emeralds in the world. As a matter of fact, we have a Zambian professor in the History Department whose brother was killed in Zambia last month over a smuggling deal that went bad. The brother was an independent emerald miner who tried to bypass the government to get a better price for his rough stones.

"The Zambian government used to export its rough stones for sale on the international market; but it stopped that practice and started finishing its own emeralds inside the country, because the stones are worth so much more cut and polished. When the government stopped selling rough stones, there was enormous pressure from international gem merchants to get the stones on the Zambian black market, so smuggling went way up. About half of all the rough emeralds produced in Zambia are smuggled out of the country before the government gets them, even though the law forbids the export of rough stones. The production of emeralds at the government's largest mine, Kagem, has gone way down. Your guess is as good as mine as to whether the decline is due to smuggling or whether the mine is actually drying up."

"My wife, Carla, has a theory that the murder victims were trying to recover cultural treasures stolen from them by European imperialists," Matt suggested.

"I don't know about that; but it wouldn't hurt for you to talk to our Zambian professor, Dr. Ziwa. Unfortunately, he went to Zambia for his brother's funeral; and he hasn't returned yet."

"One of the homicide victims had some gray ash in a pouch he was carrying; and our forensics expert found the same gray powder splattered across the case holding the emerald necklace in the gem exhibit."

"Probably some sort of magic charm to get the necklace out of the case."

"They replaced the stolen necklace with a superb fake. Nobody knows how; but it was done without tripping the Smithsonian's security system."

"It looks like you have a mystery embedded in a mystery, Mr. Alexander. Who killed the men and how did they steal a $10 million emerald necklace."

"The strangest case I've had in a long time, Dr. Phelps. I've been at it three days now, and I'm no closer to finding the killer than I was the first day."

"Some things have to play themselves out, young man. They can't be forced or coerced. Give it more time."

"The problem is that I don't have much time. The pressure is on to solve this case. Can I borrow your book?"

"Of course. Just make sure you return it."

"Thanks for your help, Dr. Phelps, and for the coffee."

"Anytime, Mr. Alexander, anytime."

Matt decided to drive over to D.C. General Hospital to visit Steve Mitchell at the medical examiner's office before meeting Jake at the Smithsonian. When he got there, he found the deputy medical examiner sitting in his cluttered office eating lunch in the midst of dozens of organ specimens in formaldehyde jars.

"Good grief, Steve! How can you eat with all this crap in here!?"

"Never underestimate our ability to accommodate ourselves to exceptional conditions, Matt. Given the right set of circumstances, I might be forced to eat what's in the jars. It's been done before."

"Don't make me gag, man. It's bad enough watching you eat that sandwich."

"Human beings are adaptable creatures. It's probably one of the best and worst traits we have. Keeps the homicide division in business, when you think about it."

"There's no way I could get used to your job, man."

"Yes, you could. It's all a question of necessity. You're more sensitive than I am, but not much more, because most people couldn't do your job."

Matt opened a window to get some fresh air.

"I read your preliminary post-mortem report, Steve. It doesn't tell me much."

"Not much to tell. They were both shot to death. I haven't finished the specimen tests yet; but all the bullets were recovered and sent to Sam. Both men were healthy, and both of them were young. One of them had just begun to cut his wisdom teeth. We finished the dental X-rays today."

Steve finished his sandwich and tossed the X-ray envelope across the desk to Matt.

"The younger one had a nearly perfect set of teeth, just two fillings. The older one, though, had extensive dental work, including root canals on three teeth and gold caps on six."

"How old do you think they are?"

"The younger one is probably 18 or 19 years old. The older one could be as much as 25. I think it's more likely that he's 22 or 23. You identify them yet?"

"No such luck. Sam is trying to match their prints against the federal print registry."

"Nobody at the Smithsonian knows them?"

"That's the story they're telling."

"I guess we're talking about long-term storage, then."

"I hope not, Steve; but this case isn't going anywhere if I can't identify the victims," Matt concluded as he walked toward the door.

"It won't be the first time," Steve replied as Matt left his office.

Matt spent the driving time to the museum thinking about the investigation and why he hadn't kicked it into high gear. His failure to identify the victims loomed large on the list of obstacles to solving the case quickly. Failing to identify the victims right off meant that he couldn't hone in on their motives for stealing the necklace or on the shooter's motive for killing them. The collective denial of museum staff members to either knowing the victims or seeing them the night of the homicides pointed away from a murderer inside the Museum of Natural History; but Matt was not so easily swayed. The lack of any apparent signs of breaking and entering that Tuesday night pointed toward an accomplice inside the museum who had probably let the victims in after closing hours.

When he arrived at the museum, Matt found Captain Bryant and Jake already interrogating staff. Bryant checked his watch as Matt walked by.

"What's happening?" Matt asked his partner.

"The same old seventy-six," Jake replied. "Nobody knows nothing about nothing."

"You haven't gotten a bite from anybody?"

"There was one old black guy in maintenance kept contradicting himself, but my guess is that he isn't hitting on all six cylinders."

"What's his name?"

"Jimmy Wilson. He works maintenance on the day-shift."

"I'll talk to him myself. Did they detail Earl Simms to us again?"

"Yeah. He just went upstairs to round up more staff."

"Have you seen Kendricks or Brandt today?"

"Yeah, Brandt was here earlier. He told me he was going over to the Castle to meet with Kendricks at one o'clock."

"I need to meet with Kendricks, myself," Matt said before leaving the museum for the Castle. Brandt and Kendricks were concluding their meeting when Matt arrived.

"What can I do for you, lieutenant?"

"I wanted to run a few loose ends by you, Kendricks."

"Like what?"

"Like how did two young black men cripple a $5 million security system and steal one of the most expensive necklaces in your gem collection?"

"I thought you were supposed to tell me that, lieutenant."

"It's your security system, not mine. When you unlocked the gem exhibit on Wednesday, it took three codes to open that door. Then the gem curator had to enter a separate code for the back of the case in addition to opening an intricate combination lock, just to get to the necklace. How did the homicide victims get the codes and the combination lock?"

"They couldn't have gotten the codes. Our security system is set up so no one knows all three codes, including me."

"That's just my point, Kendricks. If you don't know the codes, how the hell did they get them?"

"I've never told anyone what my code is, Lieutenant Alexander. Brandt and Dr. Hughes haven't, either."

"How can you be certain nobody knows all three

codes?"

"The codes are randomly generated by computer. They also contain our personal identification numbers, which are sequenced randomly among the other numbers. We're supposed to memorize the codes; there is no hard copy anywhere. After the coding sequence is complete, the entire routine is automatically deleted by the computer. The security company doesn't even know what the codes are. Even if one of us did make a hard copy, how could two strangers have gotten access to all of our codes at the same time?"

"So what happens if somebody forgets their code?"

"We have to call the security company, so they can re-initialize the computerized coding routine. Then everybody gets new codes."

"How often are the codes changed?"

"Twice a year."

"How long has this system been in place?"

"For the past five years; and we haven't had any trouble with it until now. The company that installed the security system came out to investigate the theft yesterday. They insisted that the system hadn't been breached, got pretty nasty about it, too, which means if we insist that the system was breached, they're going to defend themselves legally. I don't know where that will lead; but for now, we went ahead and changed the codes."

"If the system wasn't breached, that means that somebody gave all three codes and the combination to the lock to the homicide victims."

"That's impossible, lieutenant. I'll stake my life on

the fact that nobody knows my code but me."

"Be careful what you promise, Kendricks. Somebody has already killed twice."

Matt spent the next hour questioning the Smithsonian's director of security. When he returned to the Museum of Natural History, he went upstairs to Fisher's third floor office.

"What is it now, lieutenant?"

"More of the same, Fisher."

"I've already told you everything I know."

"Let's try this, for starters. How could the homicide victims bypass your security system? When we went into the gem exhibit on Wednesday, it took four security codes to open the door. Where did the victims get those codes?"

"I don't know how they got them!" Dr. Fisher angrily replied. "Security is Kendricks' business, not mine."

"Security in the Museum of Natural History is your business, Fisher. Has the museum's security system been breached before?"

"No, never. It's state-of-the-art. We paid a fortune for it."

"If it's so reliable, how was the necklace stolen?"

"I wasn't there when it happened. Why is everyone acting like I'm personally responsible for this situation? I run a tight ship at the Museum of Natural History. Everyone on the Mall knows that. We've haven't had a major incident of any kind in the museum since I've been director. But all of that doesn't amount to a hill of beans now. The bastards were killed in Natural History, and I have to take the fall for the Smithsonian."

As hard as Matt tried, he couldn't summon any sympathy for the man.

"They had to know the codes, Fisher. They couldn't have stolen the necklace without them."

"If those men knew the codes, the information had to come from Hughes, Brandt, or Kendricks. I'm putting my money on Kendricks."

"Why, because he's black?"

"No, not because he black. Because he's the security director; and if anyone knew all three codes, he did."

"Kendricks swears no one knew all three codes."

"That's what the security company says, too. They say their computer protocols are fail-safe; and they're willing to go to court to prove it."

"By the way," Matt said as he prepared to leave, "do you have any staff members from Zaire, Angola, or the Congo Republic?"

"I'm not aware of any; but you'll have to check with personnel to be sure."

Matt cornered Chief Brandt in his first floor office. He spent the next hour questioning Brandt about museum security procedures, especially those on the second and third-shifts. Brandt was more accessible than either Kendricks or Fisher, but Matt got no closer to finding out how the homicide victims got the security codes.

Brandt was firm in his conviction that Joe Henderson had been sleeping off a drunk the night of the murders, since that was his usual custom when he came to work with a "toot" on. Brandt accused Henderson of gross dereliction of duty and promised Matt that Henderson would certainly be fired this time. Matt wondered if Henderson was being scapegoated for the murders and the theft of the emerald necklace.

Meanwhile, back at Fourth District Headquarters, Captain Bryant rushed into the building from the parking lot to keep a four o'clock appointment with Commander Cullison.

"Come on in, Bryant. I'll be with you as soon as I sign these manual warrants."

"Take your time, sir. I've got plenty of time," Bryant assured Lloyd, who placed the completed warrants in his out box.

"So what's the deal down at the Smithsonian?"

"Alexander has pissed everybody off, including Secretary Marshall. He's throwing his weight around like a bull in a china shop."

"Are they cooperating with him?"

"Yes, sir, especially Colonel Kendricks; but Alexander's been riding Kendricks' back the hardest of all. He accused Kendricks of tampering with the security tapes before he turned them over. Kendricks swears he turned those tapes over to Alexander sight unseen."

"It's pretty easy to alter videotapes, Bryant. Don't they have a video lab down there?"

"Yes, sir, they do; but I don't believe they're stupid enough to alter those tapes. Colonel Kendricks has been playing it pretty straight with us, if you ask me. They let Alexander use an assistant director's office for interrogating staff. Sergeant Jackson is using Willis Brandt's office, and he's the chief of security for the Museum of

Natural History. Alexander is too damned particular, if you ask me."

"The pressure from downtown is on, Bryant; and that press conference Secretary Marshall put on didn't help us worth a damn. He should have kept his mouth shut and let the DCPD handle the press."

"Colonel Kendricks tried to get him to cancel the press conference, sir. Kendricks says that the only reason the secretary went ahead with it is because Alexander pissed him off so bad."

"Since when is an investigating officer required to please the goddamned secretary of the Smithsonian?"

"That's not all, Commander. Kendricks says that Alexander threatened to arrest him and Chief Brandt."

"I told him to cut Kendricks some slack."

"It's overkill, commander. Alexander likes to throw his weight around, strutting and preening like he's the commander of Fourth District Headquarters instead of you."

Lloyd gave Bryant a curious look. For his part, Bryant tried to look as pure as the driven snow while he trashed his junior officer.

"Kendricks told me that Alexander went over to the secretary's office on Wednesday afternoon and burst right into a meeting of Secretary Marshall's without knocking."

Lloyd laughed out loud.

"I guess that was a first for the secretary."

"Alexander got real nasty with the secretary when they told him they were going to put the emerald necklace in the vault. Kendricks said they can't protect the necklace if it's not in the vault or on display in the gem exhibit."

"Thanks for bringing me up to date, Bryant. I have another meeting coming up soon. Keep me informed." Lloyd yawned as he looked at his watch.

"Yes, sir. I figured you needed to know what was going on," Bryant mumbled as he left Lloyd's office.

Back in his office at the museum, Matt read the notes Jake had taken earlier after questioning Jimmy Wilson. Wilson showed up several minutes later, twisting a greasy cap in his hands.

"You Lieutenant Alexander? They said you wanted to see me."

"That's right. Come on in and sit down, Mr. Wilson."

Jimmy crept through the door and slunk over to one of the armchairs in front of the desk.

"I've been reading the statement you gave Sergeant Jackson, Mr. Wilson. You seem to have trouble figuring out where you were Wednesday morning. Is there a problem?"

"No, sir. There ain't no problem, cause I wasn't nowhere near that diorama when they was shot."

"Nobody said you were, Mr. Wilson. But it looks like you don't know where you were after you arrived at work Wednesday morning. First you said you were downstairs mopping the Associates Court dining area on the first floor. Then you changed that and said you were cleaning the bathrooms on the first floor. Then you changed that and said you were mopping the rotunda on the second floor. So which is it?"

"Aah . . . it's hard to remember where I was, lieutenant. I works on both them floors. Sometimes I'm on the first floor and sometimes I'm on the second floor."

"You can't be on both floors at the same time, Mr. Wilson. So where were you right after you came to work on Wednesday morning?"

"I went to the maintenance supply room to fetch my cart right after I clocked in. No, no, I didn't. I stopped in the employee cafeteria and had a cup of coffee. Then I went and fetched my cart."

"So what did you do after you got your cart?"

Jimmy squirmed in his chair and twisted his greasy cotton cap even tighter.

"I walks over to the Associates Dining Court, that's one of my areas, and I starts mopping the floor. Whenever I mop in there I puts all the chairs up on the tables first so I can do a good job."

"You're lying, Wilson. You didn't go anywhere near the Associates Dining Court after you came in Wednesday. You went upstairs to mop the Africa exhibit. That's when you found those murder victims in the diorama, didn't you?"

"I didn't do no such a thing. I'm telling you the gospel truth about where I was, Lieutenant Alexander."

"I don't have to take your word for it, Mr. Wilson. All I have to do is check with your supervisor to see which area of the museum is assigned to you Wednesday morning."

Matt almost felt sorry for Jimmy, who looked like

his best friend had just died.

"All right, all right. I did go upstairs to mop the exhibit. I does it twice a week on Monday and Wednesday. Well, there I was mopping all by myself, working my way back toward the diorama when I looks up and spots those two bodies. Lord have mercy! I nearly jumps out of my skin when I saw them over there with their privates all open like that. It was a terrible shock, lieutenant. It was more than I could bear, Lord knows it was. After that, I grabs my mop bucket and gets out of there as fast as my legs would carry me."

"Did you report the bodies to security?"

"I was too scared to report it. I was shaking and shivering like I had seen a ghost. So I goes down to the first aid room and lays down on the sofa to calm myself."

"When did you get around to reporting it, Mr. Wilson?"

"I laid down for a while until I felt strong enough to get up. I was still scared and shaking from the shock. I was gonna tell somebody, honest I was. Then them tourist ladies from Canada found the bodies and there wasn't no point in me getting myself mixed up in all that trouble, too."

"Was that the only reason you didn't report seeing the bodies Wednesday morning?"

"Well, I tries to avoid trouble, lieutenant; but things ain't been right around here lately. What's been happening don't set well with me, but there wasn't nothing I could do about it."

"What do you mean, Mr. Wilson? What things haven't

been right around here?"

"Don't make me tell you, lieutenant. They'll hurt me for sure if they find out I turned them in to the police," Jimmy pleaded.

"Nobody's going to hurt you, Mr. Wilson. I'll see to that. If you don't tell me what's going on, I'll have to arrest you for withholding evidence."

Jimmy cringed and wrung his greasy cap even tighter.

"Have mercy, Jesus! They gon kill me for sure."

"Nobody is going to kill you, Mr. Wilson. Get control of yourself and tell me what happened."

"Round bout three months ago, I was working a double shift on account of we was short staffed 'cause some of the maintenance people was on vacation. I was in the supply room on t'other side of the lockers when two maintenance people comes in from second-shift. They don't know I'm there, you see, cause I don't never work the second-shift. Anyways, I hears them talking about how to get some people into the museum after it closes, people who wasn't supposed to be in here. They says they might do it this way and then again they might do it that way. They was figgering which way was best, because they didn't want to be caught. I was scared to death that they would find out I was on t'other side of the lockers, so I was quiet as a mouse. Well, they finally left and I creeped out to the hall to see who t'was.

"Who were they?"

"Kofi Asante and Carlos Williams."

"What did you do after that?"

"I was scared. Kofi and Carlos are troublemakers. They real mean, too."

"So, you didn't do anything about it?"

"Yeah, I did. I told Mr. Henry Hughes about what I overheard. Well, when he asks Kofi and Carlos about it, the two of them deny every word. Then, they threatens to kill me if I ever mention their names again."

"What was done about it?"

"Nary thing did they do. Mr. Hughes says it's their word against mine, so he drops it on the spot and tells me not to come to him with any more hearsay. He don't want no trouble with them two, believe me."

"Menacing is a crime, Mr. Wilson. You can press charges if they're threatening you."

"No, sir! They ain't bothered me no more, and I don't want to press no charges."

"That's all for now, Mr. Wilson. Don't worry about Asante and Williams. I'll take care of them."

Jimmy Wilson threw Matt a frightened look as he left the office. Matt mulled over Jimmy's story while looking through the list of staff members already interviewed, and neither Kofi Asante or Carlos Williams showed up. He asked Earl Simms to make certain that he brought both Asante and Williams directly to him after they clocked in for second-shift. Then he paid Henry Hughes a visit.

CHAPTER 7

Hughes' reception was cool.

"I just finished talking to Jimmy Wilson, Hughes."

"So what does any of this have to do with me?"

"Jimmy Wilson says he overheard two other maintenance men plotting to let some unauthorized people into the museum after hours and that he reported the incident to you."

"I don't remember him reporting anything to me."

"Why would he lie about that?"

"He's liar and a thief, lieutenant. Just last year, he was caught stealing meat from the refrigerated locker in the associates' dining room. The only reason I remember the name is that we discussed the incident in our weekly staff meeting. I'll bet he didn't tell you about that, did he?"

"No, he didn't mention it."

"The only reason we kept him on is that Secretary Marshall didn't have the guts to authorize firing him."

"Williams swears he told you about the conversation he overheard between Kofi Asante and Carlos Williams; and that after you confronted them with it, they backed you down and you decided to drop it."

"That's not true. Kofi and Carlos are troublemakers.

They go around the museum race-baiting and stirring up trouble among the blacks, but they never backed me down because I'm not afraid of them."

"Have it your own way, Hughes. Maybe you can explain how two young black men got past your security system and stole that necklace?"

"I don't know how they did it."

"Kendricks explained your security system to me, and it's damned near impossible for anybody outside the museum to breach that system without inside help."

"So, why are you asking me about it? Wally Kendricks is over security."

"You control two of the codes for the gem exhibit; and you also had the combination to the lock on the case holding the emerald necklace."

"I can't use my code or the combination unless Willis Brandt and Wally Kendricks are there. You saw that when we opened the case on Wednesday."

"Somebody bypassed the museum's security system, Hughes; and I'm not buying some bullshit about two black men greased to the gills, dressed up like African tribesmen taking out the best security system money can buy with some voodoo. They had to have help from inside the museum."

"Voodoo! What's this about voodoo?"

"What do you think the homicide victims were all greased up and flinging dust all over the place for? It's nothing but a smokescreen, Hughes. Whoever stole that necklace breached the museum's security system, and they didn't do it with any damned voodoo, either."

"If that's all, lieutenant, I have work to do."

"Yeah, right," Matt replied as he left Henry Hughes' office.

When he returned to the first floor, he found Kofi Asante and Carlos Williams waiting for him. Kofi was tall, slim, and light-skinned enough to pass for white. He had hazel eyes and long curly hair, which he wore in a ponytail. Carlos was built like a boxer, short, dark, and intense-looking. Both men looked grim at the prospect of being questioned.

"Come in, Mr. Asante."

Kofi gave Carlos a smug glance before walking into the office.

"I thought you wanted to talk to both of us."

"That's right, but I question suspects one at a time."

"Suspects! What do you mean, suspects!?"

"Oops, a slip of the tongue, Asante. You're not suspected of anything you didn't do."

"I haven't done anything, man. Don't you even pretend you got something on me."

"Have a seat."

"I prefer to stand up if you don't mind."

"What's your job at the museum, Asante?"

"I'm a janitor. The museum says we're housekeeping personnel, but I'm nothing more than a glorified janitor just the same. I do all the heavy lifting and backbreaking work around here. That's my job, Lieutenant Alexander."

"You don't seem to like it much."

"I didn't get my bachelor's degree from UDC to move

exhibits around."

"How long you worked here?"

"Fifteen years. I thought I could improve my life with a degree, but all that crap about a college education is nothing but a scam. You can't do any better than the white man lets you."

"You must be making pretty good money if you've been in the Civil Service system for 15 years."

"For a janitor, you mean."

"For a bachelor's degree, I mean."

"I'm tapped out at my grade level. I'll never get another raise if I'm not promoted."

"Won't they promote you here?"

"These racist mother . . . No, Lieutenant Alexander, they won't promote me. Don't you recognize the last bastion of white cultural supremacy when you're sitting in it, man?"

"I suppose that's one name for it, Asante."

"It's nothing but a slave plantation in here. The only difference is that the niggers can read and write and occasionally speak up for themselves. The trouble is, they don't listen to a word we have to say."

"The Smithsonian has been hiring blacks a long time, Asante. Paul Davis is a museum director, and Wallace Kendricks is Director of Security. I understand they have a black assistant secretary, too."

"There are two kinds of black folk, lieutenant. The kind who have knowledge of themselves as the original Asiatic black man who came out of Africa with true knowledge of self and God; and the kind that accepts the evil degradation of the white man's system and have no knowledge of self and God. Paul Davis and Wallace Kendricks are puppets of the white regime at the Smithsonian, especially Kendricks who underneath it all really thinks he's a white man. He runs around the Smithsonian taking care of unruly niggers for the white folk. His title is director of security, but his real job is keeping niggers in line when they get fed up with sweeping floors, slopping mops, slinging hash, and cleaning toilets. Kendricks takes care of their business better than they do. And they despise him worse than they do the rest of us, because he actually believes he's refined his manners and polished himself off enough to pass among them without being called a nigger. Wallace Kendricks is a very bad joke."

"How can you dislike a place so much and continue to work here?"

"Because I have as much right to work here as Secretary Marshall. I pay federal taxes just like he does and it's my taxes that pay his salary. Every black man in this country has a right to a decent job so he can support his family just like white men do. But they put half of us in prison, while the rest of us are forced to beg on the streets, or shoot up coke or heroin in an alley, or gang bang in the ghetto. Yeah, I work here and here I'll stay until I get good and damned ready to leave."

"Let's get to the point, Asante. Did you work this past Tuesday?"

"Yeah, I was at work on Tuesday."

"What time did you leave the museum that day?"

"I left at midnight, my regular time."

"Did you put in any overtime on Tuesday?"

"No, I didn't."

"Did you return to the museum after you left?"

"No, I didn't come back. I went straight home, and you can check with my wife if you don't believe me. I was home the rest of the night."

"I will check with her, Asante."

"Be my guest. I got nothing to hide."

"I understand you had a run-in with Henry Hughes a while back."

"Who's been blabbing my business to you?"

"Did you have a run-in with Hughes?"

"Yeah, I put a hurting on him, but good. He accused me of dereliction of duty; and when I told him he was telling a racist lie, he had the nerve to get up in my face and push me around. That's when I grabbed his intellectual behind and turned him every which way but loose. Then the creep went and filed a complaint against me for assault and battery, couldn't take his whipping like a man. He actually wanted Kendricks to call the District Police and have me arrested. They didn't have a leg to stand on, because the dummy attacked me in front of three other janitors. They wrote me a reprimand and put it in my file, but they couldn't do anything else. Now when he sees me coming, he hurries the other side of the hall." Kofi laughed out loud.

"Henry Hughes says you and Carlos are race-baiters and troublemakers and that you go around the museum stirring up the black workers."

"He would see it that way. I'm High Priest of the Ife Temple, lieutenant. I spread the word of God to black people at the museum who haven't been totally corrupted by the white man's evil. Some of us are still willing to listen when I bring the word of God to them."

"Just what is the Ife Temple, Asante?"

"It's a spiritual center where we teach the religion of the one true God, the religion of the original people of God, the black Egyptians who called their land Khem and called themselves Khemites. Their temples weren't like the white man's churches, lieutenant, where people go to worship for an hour on Sunday and forget about God for the rest of the week. Egyptian temples were total spiritual centers where learning and spirituality were combined into the only life-giving system of knowledge in the world, given to the Khemites by the original God of the Asiatic black man, Amun-Ra. In ancient times, anyone who wanted knowledge had to go down into black Egypt to get it. They all went to Egypt to be educated, including Jesus Christ, Plato, and Alexander the Great. Alexander the Great's mama was a priestess of Amun-Ra and she brought her son up in her faith. He asked to be buried in Egypt, because he believed in the original God of our fathers, Amun-Ra."

"That's all very interesting, Asante, but I was told that you and your friend Carlos were overheard plotting to sneak people into the museum after hours."

"That's a lie."

"So you deny having that conversation with Carlos Williams?"

"Yes, I deny it. Henry Hughes has been out to get me and Carlos ever since I whipped his butt. He made that lie up to get me in trouble."

Matt was confused by the fact that both Kofi Asante and Henry Hughes deny that the incident described by Jimmy Wilson ever took place. If they were telling the truth, Jimmy would have to be lying; and Matt couldn't see why Jimmy would make up such a lie.

"I guess you know that two black men were killed in the museum early Wednesday morning, Asante."

"Yeah, I heard about it."

"How do you think they got into the museum?"

"Why you asking me how they got in here?"

"I thought you might have an opinion."

"I'm just maintenance around here, lieutenant. My opinions don't count."

"I'd like to hear what you have to say, anyway."

"What I say is that Wallace Kendricks messed up big time. I don't know how they got in here; but I don't see how that butt-kissing Uncle Tom is going to keep his job after this."

"Kendricks says they didn't break into the museum, because they didn't trip any of the alarms. If they didn't break in, somebody on the inside must have let them in."

"Well, no matter how they got in here, lieutenant, it don't have nothing to do with me. My name is Bennett and I ain't in it."

"Can you think of anyone at the Smithsonian who might be in it?"

"No, I can't."

"That's all for now, Asante."

Kofi quickly left the office, and Carlos reluctantly took his place. Like Kofi, Carlos hotly denied Jimmy Wilson's allegation. Matt talked to him for 30 minutes, but Carlos was sullen and close-mouthed. He revealed very little about his relationships within the museum, especially with Henry Hughes. After Carlos left, Jake entered the office and flopped into a chair.

"I've had it, partner."

Matt leaned back in his chair and propped his feet on the desk.

"Same here, man."

"Did you find out anything else from Jimmy Wilson?"

"He admitted that he was the first one to find the homicide victims on Wednesday morning. He found them before the Canadian women."

"That so? Why didn't he report it?"

"Says he was too scared. When he finally screwed up his nerve, the Canadian women had already sounded the alarm. What do you know about the Ife Temple, Jake?"

"That commune over on Fourteenth Street?"

"Commune? Kofi Asante said it was a church, and he was the high priest."

Jake laughed out loud. "High priest, my granny's fanny. From what I hear, a lot of stuff goes down at the Ife Temple, partner; and ain't none of it high."

"How so?"

"Well, it's supposed to be a church, but all of the so-called priests got as many wives as they want; and when you drive by that place it looks like a baby farm from behind that high fence. Ain't no birth control never been nowhere near the Ife Temple."

"Does it have a rap sheet downtown?"

"Naw. The word on the street is they smoke much dope in there, but they ain't selling it. They hell on some crackheads, though. One got into the yard a while back and somebody whipped his ass so bad they had to take him to the hospital."

"Was anybody arrested?"

"You kidding? They don't do no talking to the police at the Ife Temple, partner. Women just like they mute, and ain't but two or three of the men allowed to say anything. If they're messed up in this case, you got a serious problem."

"Nothing I can't handle. Jimmy Wilson says he overheard Kofi and Carlos plotting to sneak somebody into the museum after hours."

"So what do they have to say for themselves?"

"They deny it."

"Do you think Jimmy Wilson's lying?"

"Who knows? Seems if Jimmy was going to make up a lie, it wouldn't be as elaborate as the story he told me. He seems kind of low in the imagination department. I want you to check with personnel to get Jimmy Wilson's overtime schedule for the past six months, Jake. He says he was working a double shift the night he overheard Kofi and Carlos plotting."

"It'll have to wait until tomorrow. Personnel is closed for the day."

"That's fine. I'm on my way back to headquarters, anyway. Is Bryant still here?"

"You kidding? He's been gone for five hours."

"Typical."

"Man, you ought to call it a night like me. Let's go to Lacy's for a drink," Jake urged.

"Can't tonight, man. I'm on my way home. Then I have to get that report ready for Lloyd's 10 o'clock meeting tomorrow."

Matt opened the front door to his house 30 minutes later.

"Daddy! Daddy! Daddy! You're home, Daddy!" five-year-old Jenny screamed as she dove into her father's arms from the stairs. Matt had to drop everything he was carrying to catch her.

"Daddy! You're home, Daddy!" three-year-old Robbie repeated as he grabbed his father's right leg.

"Jenny, I told you not to jump off the stairs like that when I have something in my hands. The next time you do it, I'm not going to catch you."

"Daddy, make Robbie stop saying everything I say."

"Daddy! Daddy! Daddy!" Robbie continued to chant as he hung on to his father's leg.

"You're his big sister, Jenny. He admires you. That's why he repeats everything you say," Matt replied as he kissed Jenny, put her down, and picked his son up.

"I don't want him to 'mire' me, Daddy. I want him to stop saying what I say. He can talk all by himself."

"Imitation is the sincerest form of flattery, Jenny. What have you been doing all day, little man?"

"I made cookies and I played dolls with Jenny, Daddy."

"You did what?" Matt exclaimed as he walked into the kitchen where his wife Carla was washing the dinner dishes.

"Carla, when I asked Robbie what he did today, he said he made cookies and played dolls with Jenny."

"Hello, Matthew. It's good to see you, too," Carla sarcastically replied, keeping her back to her husband.

"Did you hear what I said, Carla? He played dolls all day with Jenny."

"And just what is wrong with him playing dolls with his sister?" Carla demanded as she swung around to confront her husband.

"I told you I didn't want him playing with dolls, Carla. He's got plenty of toys of his own. Why can't Jenny play with his toys sometimes?"

"Ask her yourself."

"Jenny, why don't you play with your brother's toys?"

"I don't like to play with trucks and soldiers, Daddy," Jenny explained.

"I don't like to play with trucks and soldiers, too," Robbie echoed.

"Look at this. He's turned against his own toys."

"I like to play with my Bobbie dolls, Daddy," Jenny continued.

"Me too. I like Bobbie dolls," Robbie agreed.

"What's for dinner, Carla?"

"Baked chicken," Carla barked as she slammed pots and pans into the cabinet under the stove.

Carla's sullen mood lingered past the washing up and

moved into the family room, where she sulked over a glass of wine and a magazine. Matt finished his dinner and joined her after coaxing the children upstairs with a promise to read them a bedtime story. He sat next to Carla and tried to cuddle. She pushed him away.

"What's wrong this time?"

"Isn't that the whole point, Matthew, time? If you spent more time with your children, you could make sure that Robbie played with his toys. You can't have your cake and eat it too, Detective Lieutenant Matthew Alexander."

"I don't mind him playing with dolls sometimes, Carla; but he shouldn't play with them everyday. He's a boy."

"That's quite a revelation coming from a father who's never home. If you're so concerned about your son, why don't you spend more time with him, Matthew, while he's still young enough to need you?"

"That's a low blow, Carla. You know I spend as much time with the children as I can."

"That's bullshit, Matthew. You're so wrapped up in your work you can't even see that I've had to be both mother and father to these children in addition to working 30 hours a week at the mental health center, seeing patients. I'm so tired most of the time I don't know whether I'm coming or going; and you have the nerve to come in here at seven o'clock in the evening and complain about the toys Robbie's been playing with."

"I wasn't complaining, Carla."

"Yes, dammit, you were complaining. If you're such

a good father, why don't you go upstairs and give the children their baths and put them to bed?"

"I can't tonight, honey. I have to go back to headquarters to finish a report for Lloyd on the Smithsonian homicides."

"Isn't that the way it always is, Matthew? I would if I could, but I can't, so I shan't."

"There's no point in being a smartass, Carla," Matt snapped as he grabbed his briefcase and headed for the door.

"Isn't this typical? Promise the children you'll read them a story and then run out on them."

"Goddamit, Carla. Give me some fucking space, will you!" Matt shouted as he stormed out the front door.

Carla jumped up and slammed it shut as he walked down the steps. Matt stood at the foot of the steps and looked at the door, tears in his eyes. Carla sat down on the sofa and cried. She hurriedly dried her eyes as she heard the children coming down the stairs. They ran into the kitchen looking for their father.

"Where's Daddy, Mommy? Jenny asked as she ran into the family room with one of her storybooks.

"He's gone back to work, honey."

"But Daddy promised to read me a story," Jenny cried.

"Daddy promised to read me a story," Robbie echoed.

"Give me the book. I'll read the story."

Robbie jumped into his mother's lap and tried to drink from her glass of wine.

"Is Daddy coming back home, Mommy?" Jenny asked as she snuggled into the crook of her mother's arm.

"Of course he is coming home," Carla replied as she pried the wine out of her son's grasp. "Daddy comes home every night, because he loves us."

"Daddy loves us," Robbie repeated as Carla began to read the storybook.

As he drove to headquarters, Matt felt the muscles in his neck tightening from the strain of his argument with Carla. He knew she was right. He didn't spend enough time with his children. He was the one who would have to teach his son how to be a man; his wife couldn't do that. He would also have to teach his daughter how she should expect to be treated by a man; his wife couldn't do that, either. He usually managed to keep the demons at bay, to drive his life straight ahead and avoid the road hazards, but Carla had taken him on an emotional detour, and he was deeply shaken by her anger.

She was telling him that he wasn't giving her the support she needed to avoid the road hazards in her life, that she was tired of carrying the load by herself. She was his touchstone, but he wasn't hers. He wanted to help her, but he didn't know how. When he had asked her if she wanted to quit her job, she had insisted that she loved her work and that she'd go crazy if she had to stay home with the children all day. What she wanted was more of his time, the only thing he couldn't give her.

When he arrived at headquarters, he found a message from Sam in his in-basket. Sam indicated he still hadn't identified the victims' prints, that response time for their pictures from outside jurisdictions would be slow, and that Matt shouldn't raise his hopes for identifying the victims anytime soon. Sam's news did not improve Matt's mood. Matt began work on the homicide report for Lloyd's morning meeting. While he worked at his PC, he thought about his failure to identify the victims three days after they were killed. He went over the games he knew Wallace Kendricks and the Smithsonian were playing with him while denying it to his face. He questioned the story Jimmy Wilson had told him, a story that Carlos Johnson, Kofi Asante, and Henry Hughes all hotly denied. He thought about the meeting with Lloyd planned for the next morning, a meeting he dreaded. He left Fourth District Headquarters at midnight. On the way out, he dropped a copy of the homicide report in the night box outside Lloyd's office.

When he arrived back home, he found the children asleep in bed with Carla again. He changed into his robe and slippers and went back downstairs to the family room where he put his favorite jazz CD on, made himself a stiff Maker's Mark on the rocks, and settled back into his favorite chair with Friday's copy of the *Washington Post*. Later, he heard the sound of footsteps descending the stairs. When he looked up from the paper, he found Carla standing in the doorway of the family room in the sheerest black negligee he had ever seen.

"You look gorgeous. Is that new?"

"This old thing? I've had it for ages."

"You must have been wearing it for someone else, because I've never seen you in that before. Believe me, I would remember that nightgown."

"Make me a drink, honey."

Matt gave her a skeptical look before he walked over to where she was standing.

"Are you burying the hatchet?"

"Do you see a hatchet anywhere on me?"

"No, baby. You couldn't hide anything under that gown," Matt laughed, pulling her into his arms, and giving her several soft kisses as he stroked and caressed her body.

Carla returned his kisses just as passionately. Matt pulled away first.

"I thought you wanted a drink."

"I do want a drink, honey," Carla murmured as she languidly curled her body into the arm of the sofa.

When Matt returned with Carla's drink, he softened the lights before sitting beside his wife.

"I want to talk about what happened tonight, Carla."

"Not again, honey. Let's put all that behind us."

"I can't, Carla. I need to talk about it tonight."

"I'm sorry I got so angry, Matthew. I was feeling overwhelmed."

"You know what I love about you, Carla. I love the way you're always there for me and the kids. But I get the feeling you don't think I have your back."

"You give me enough support, honey. I just need you to be around more."

"You don't really believe that, Carla. You think I'm taking you for granted."

"You're overreacting, Matthew. I can handle it."

"I know you can handle it; but you need more support,

baby. Tell me what I can do to help you."

"Are you willing to quit your job, Matthew?"

"No, Carla. I'm not willing to quit my job."

"Then what are we discussing this for if you're not willing to take a job that lets you spend more time at home?"

"You're putting me in a box, Carla. Why can't I keep my job and support you, too?"

"Because we're in a box, honey. We don't have the money to hire Mrs. Taylor to be here with the children all day, so there's nothing to be done. Besides, I can handle it."

"I don't want you to handle it, Carla. I want you to feel like you get what you need from me."

"What are we talking about, Matthew?"

"I'm talking about hiring Mrs. Taylor full time."

"You know we can't afford it."

"We will afford it. I don't know how yet, but we will."

"You know how I feel about having someone else raise our children."

"We'll still raise the children. Mrs. Taylor would cook and clean the house and babysit while you're at work; and you wouldn't have to worry about finding sitters for the kids."

"It sounds like heaven, Matthew, but it almost never works out, especially for what we can afford to pay. Besides, I don't think Mrs. Taylor would take the job full time. I just don't know about this, honey."

"We'll find someone; and I'll find a way to afford it," Matt insisted as he slipped her negligee off her shoulders and kissed her face and neck.

"She can't be young, Matthew. I won't take her unless she's old and ugly."

"If she's too old, you'll end up taking care of her," Matt laughed.

"Let's go up to bed, honey."

"Are the children in our bed?"

"Not tonight. I put them in their own beds tonight."

CHAPTER 8

"Damn, partner. It's Saturday. I was planning to sleep late this morning. What time is it, anyway?"

"Eight o'clock. I have a 10 o'clock with Lloyd in his office; and I want you to meet me at the Ife Temple at eleven-thirty."

"At the Ife Temple. What for?"

"Just curious, that's all."

"Curiosity killed the cat, man."

"Yeah, right. I'll see you there."

Matt went back upstairs to wake Carla, who was lying in bed basking in the luxuriant satisfaction that only a Saturday morning sleep-in brings. He sat on the side of the bed and stroked her naked body through the sheet. Carla murmured pleasing sounds as she roused from a deep sleep.

"Where're you going? It's Saturday, isn't it?"

"All day; I have a meeting with Lloyd at eight."

"Will you be gone all day again?"

"No. Baby, I'll be back this afternoon."

"Promises, promises." Carla turned her back to Matt and pulled the sheet under her chin.

"I said I'll be back early this afternoon, Carla, and I will."

"I'll believe it when I see you walk through the front door, Matthew."

"Come on, baby, cut me some slack," Matt pleaded as he kissed her on the neck and ear.

Carla turned a deaf ear to his plea.

"Come on, Carla. I thought I was back on my good foot."

"Your good foot is very shaky," Carla pouted, pretending to be angrier than she was.

Matt suddenly stripped the sheet from her body, pulled her into his arms, and kissed her deeply, slowly, and passionately. The sheet slid to the foot of the bed as Carla responded just as passionately. After he released her, she did a sensuous slide back on the mattress and languidly stretched her naked body.

"You have to get up, Carla. The children are downstairs eating cereal."

"Let me sleep another hour, honey."

"I'm leaving now."

When Matt went downstairs to Lloyd's office for their 10 o'clock meeting, he found that Captain Bryant had preceded him. Lloyd Cullison was already reading the homicide report Matt had delivered an hour earlier and didn't look up. Matt got himself a cup of coffee.

"This is the damnedest case I've seen in a long time, Alexander. You haven't even ID'd the victims yet."

"You don't have to tell me that, Lloyd."

"Somebody needs to tell you that you haven't moved this case off square one. Just what the hell have you been doing all week?"

A slow, very intense burn crept up Matt's neck and face as he concentrated on staying calm, his best defense against Lloyd's brutal tactics. He had learned the hard way that keeping cool gave him an advantage with a commander who used his subordinates' anger to decimate them.

"I've worked this case the same way I work all my cases, Lloyd. You don't get the best hit rate in the homicide division by sitting on your ass watching your fingernails grow."

"You started this case Wednesday. It's Saturday, and you still haven't identified the victims and don't have a clue as to who the goddamned shooter is or why he killed the victims and didn't take the freaking emerald necklace. Just pardon me if I don't congratulate you for solving more cases than anybody else. You haven't solved this case; and Chief Carter is all over my ass because the mayor and the D.C. representative are all over his ass. What am I supposed to tell the chief when I meet with him today? 'We don't know jack shit about the homicide investigation, chief; but Matthew Alexander is the best detective on the force, so you can rest easy.'"

Bryant smirked in contempt as Lloyd poured it on.

"I didn't ask for this case, Lloyd; and I don't need this grief. You'd be doing me a favor if you assigned it to somebody else."

"You don't get off that easy, hotshot. It's your case, and by God, you'll see it through to the end. Now, tell me what the hell is going on down there."

"Wallace Kendricks and Willis Brandt have been one

step ahead of us since we started. I told you they made copies of the video tapes; and they questioned the third-shift guards before we could get to them. They know how that security system was taken out, too. It has to be an inside job. There's no way anyone could break into the Smithsonian, disable a $5 million security system, and steal a $10 million emerald necklace without inside help."

"Can you prove any of what you know, lieutenant?"

"Not yet."

"What the hell am I supposed to tell Chief Carter?"

"Whatever you like, Lloyd."

"You hear that, Captain Bryant? I'm trying to make sense out of his half-assed investigation, and he smarts off at me."

"Is that all? I have work to do," Matt said as he rose to leave.

"Hell no, it's not all. Since you're the one who dropped the ball on this case, I want you in my meeting with the Chief. I'm not taking the rap for this pile of bullshit by myself."

"What time is the meeting?"

"One o'clock in the chief's office."

"I'll be there," Matt replied as he left the meeting.

"Make damned sure you're not late," Lloyd shouted after him.

"It's just like I told you, sir. He's doing a half-assed job on this case."

"He's done a good investigation, Bryant. The Smithsonian is trying to save their ass with the press and on Capitol Hill."

"Kendricks wouldn't try to cover for the Smithsonian, would he?"

"I've known Wallace Kendricks a long time, Bryant. He didn't get to be a colonel in the army by bucking the system. He's a team player. Alexander's right. He's carrying the Smithsonian's water, no question in my mind about that. I just wonder how far he'll go for them."

"Alexander has already accused him of tampering with evidence."

"I hope not, for Wally Kendricks' sake."

When Matt arrived at the Ife Temple, he found Jake waiting for him across the street. Matt sized up the exterior of the temple, noting its three stories of white brick with black trim. The grass and shrubbery around the house were conspicuously green compared to the mostly barren dirt yards of the neighboring tenements. The temple was surrounded by a six-foot fence and had a large sign mounted over the front door which read "IFE TEMPLE" above an outline of the Eye of Ra and a banner that read "ENTER HERE ALL YOU WHO SEEK WISDOM AND TRUTH" below the eye. Matt scanned the run-down neighborhood around the temple with its corner liquor stores, trash-filled alleys, drug addicts, and panhandlers. The street was lined with trash and several abandoned grocery carts. Matt also noticed a steady stream of people dressed in African-style clothes being admitted into the temple by two men stationed inside the front door.

After showing their badges, the two detectives were admitted to the temple by reluctant doormen. Matt asked to speak to Kofi Asante. He and Jake were ordered by the younger of the two sentries to remove their shoes and leave them in an alcove near the front door. The older sentry ushered Matt and Jake into a large room filled with the temple faithful sitting on the floor atop rugs and cushions, men on one side, women on the other. The guard pointed Matt and Jake to two cushions at the rear of the men's side.

Kofi Asante was sitting on a raised platform at the front of the room in a throne-like wooden chair, his hands resting on carved lion heads jutting from the arms of the chair. He was dressed in a long, white caftan and matching skull cap over flowing, shoulder length hair. Carlos Williams was sitting on Kofi's right. A tall fair-skinned woman sat on Kofi's left. Both Carlos and the woman were also dressed in white. The sound of children's voices filtered into the room from the upper reaches of the temple.

Matt scanned the meeting room and noted that most of the temple's worshippers were young men and women who were mesmerized by Kofi's voice. They signified their agreement with Kofi by vigorously nodding their heads and saying "Amen, Iman" or "That's right, Iman." Kofi looked regal sitting on his carved throne, surrounded by his faithful followers hanging on his every word. Neither Matt nor Jake could miss the Eye of Ra on the wall behind Kofi or the Egyptian statues that decorated the meeting room.

"Man, that don't even look like the same dude we questioned yesterday," Jake whispered to Matt.

"It's him all right," Matt replied as he listened more intently to what Kofi was saying.

"When they stole us from Africa in chains, they stripped away our true knowledge of self and God. After they brought us to these foreign shores, they tore us away from our kinsmen who spoke the same language. They put us with Africans who didn't speak the same tongue or practice the same customs, because they didn't want our culture to survive. They stripped us naked physically, mentally, and culturally, brothers and sisters. They wanted us to forget who we were and where we came from. Hear my words! They wanted us to forget our ancestors, our traditions, our history. But most of all, they wanted us to forget the one true God of our fathers who shows us the path of righteousness here on earth and the path to eternal peace and happiness after we leave this earth.

"That's why black people all over America are confused and lost, brothers and sisters. We're abusing our babies, killing each other, fighting and destroying each other, putting poison up our noses and in our veins, selling that same poison to our children, disrespecting our elders, our spouses, ourselves. Doing any degrading, whorish thing . . . anything to make the white man's dollar. We have never been so low, even in the deepest, darkest, depths of slavery. We have never been so low. We have no knowledge of ourselves as the original Asiatic black man from whom all other people have come. We were first and we will be last. Make no mistake about that, my brothers and sisters; we will be last.

"We have no knowledge of ourselves. Our women carry themselves like sluts and harlots, displaying their bodies like meat in a butcher's window. A woman's body is a temple. A woman should be covered from head to foot when she leaves her home. Her body is not to be seen or coveted for pleasure by anyone but her husband. Our women have no shame, brothers and sisters. They parade themselves through the streets like prostitutes. And when men disrespect and dishonor them, they have the nerve to be offended, with their low-cut, skin-tight dresses and pants. Our men are no better. They impregnate our women, walk away, and never look back at the innocent children they have brought into the world. Our men have created a generation of fatherless children, children abused by their mothers or their mothers' boyfriends. Helpless children who need love and discipline. Children who need their fathers to help them grow up to be men and women."

Jake complained about sitting on the floor after Kofi finished preaching 20 minutes later. Kofi waited on the platform while Carlos and the woman passed the collection plates. Then he mingled with his congregation. The members of the temple heaped praise and admiration on him as he basked in their adulation. Kofi eventually worked his way through the crowd to the back of the room where Matt and Jake waited for him.

"What did you think of my teaching, Lieutenant Alexander?"

"You get no complaints from me, Asante."

"What about you, sergeant?"

"Is this what you call church?"

"Our main service isn't until noon. The talk you just heard is called a Teaching. We hold them every morning before the temple service. I do the Teachings on Saturday and Sunday. Other members of the temple teach during the week."

"How long has the Ife Temple been operating?" Matt asked.

"I started the temple 15 years ago. There were just a few of us for a long time, but my congregation has grown over the years."

"How many members do you have, Asante?"

"Over 300, lieutenant."

"How many live in this house?"

"Why do you want to know that?" Kofi demanded.

"The word on the street is that all the men in the house have multiple wives. Is that true?"

"That's a dirty lie! Besides that, it's nobody's business how many wives we have."

The two guards manning the front door walked over to Kofi. Kofi told them everything was okay and they resumed their places beside the door.

"Bigamy is against the law, Asante."

"You have to be legally married to be a bigamist," Jake said.

"What did you come here for, lieutenant?"

"Two things, Asante. First, you and Carlos did let somebody into the museum after hours, and I'm going to prove it. Second, you better watch your step, because I'm watching every little move you make."

"Man, you too much," Kofi laughed unconvincingly.

"I'm smart enough to have your number, chump."

"Lieutenant, why do you come to my temple bringing confusion and hostility? I don't have time for this ignorance," Kofi angrily replied, leaving the two detectives in the alcove as he returned to his flock.

Matt and Jake left the Ife Temple under the hostile glare of the two sentries, who continued to watch them as they stood outside Matt's car talking.

"What was that all about?" Jake asked.

"A long shot."

"You think he's the shooter?"

"Maybe. Shit, who knows? I decided to push his buttons, because he and Carlos were up to something. Jimmy Wilson wasn't lying on them."

"That was three months ago, partner."

"You take what you can get, Jake. I don't have jack shit on anybody else over there."

"Where you on your way to now?" Jake asked as Matt got under the wheel.

"I have a meeting with Lloyd and Chief Carter at one."

"Man, you can't get downtown in five minutes."

"Wanna bet?" Matt asked as he screeched away from the curb.

Matt arrived at Chief Carter' office several minutes late. Lloyd checked his watch and gave his subordinate a hostile glare when he entered the chief's office.

"The Medical Examiner's report says they were smeared with palm oil; and that one of them had bone ash under the fingernails of his right hand. It says they had some chicken bones on them, too. What do you make of that, Lieutenant Alexander?" Chief Carter asked Matt as soon as he sat down.

"I didn't know what to make of it, sir. So I took one of the African costumes they were wearing over to Dr. Anthony Phelps at Howard University. He's an expert on African tribal customs."

"So what'd he have to say?"

"He said that the oil was used to protect the men from evil spirits; and that the ashes and chicken bones were used to cast a magic spell."

"So what does that have to do with the homicides?" the chief asked Matt.

"They were practicing voodoo, sir. Dr. Phelps said that it's not unusual for Africans to use magic potions and charms in their rituals."

"Not unusual if they were African-Americans, either," the chief replied. "You'd be surprised at how many people believed in voodoo where I grew up in Shelby County, Alabama. Most folks in my neighborhood were scared to death of somebody putting some conjure on them."

"You don't believe any of that mumbo-jumbo, do you, chief?" Lloyd asked with a smirk.

"Let's say I have a healthy skepticism, commander. I don't practice it, but I don't discount it, either."

"I say it's hogwash. There's no way anybody could steal a $10 million necklace with voodoo," Lloyd insisted.

"What kind of security system do they have, lieutenant?" the chief asked.

Matt briefed the chief on the museum's security system.

"I agree with you, commander. It took a hell of a lot more than chicken bones and ashes to disable that security system," the chief replied. "What about the victims showing up on the security tapes? Where did they come from? And where did they go after the cameras lost them?"

"We don't know, sir. We tried to retrace their steps from where the cameras picked them up, but the first-floor corridors had been mopped by the time we got there on Wednesday. We still don't know why the cameras didn't pick them up coming back down the stairs after they executed the theft."

"So they just disappeared in a puff of smoke, huh?"

Lloyd laughed. "Maybe there's something to that voodoo after all, chief."

Chief Carter laughed, too. "Maybe that's what we need to solve this case, commander. A witch doctor. I should get him to answer questions at my next press conference."

Everybody laughed.

"So who's the shooter, lieutenant?"

"I wish I knew, sir. I'm convinced it's an inside job. Nobody at the Smithsonian admits knowing anything about the homicides; but somebody working there killed those men."

"What was their motive? They left the emerald necklace on one of the victims."

"I can't explain that, sir."

"There are very few answers in this report. The

mayor's office is all over me to solve this case. Your report does not inspire confidence, lieutenant."

"It's a tough case, Chief Carter. The Smithsonian is playing its hand close to the vest. They've tampered with the evidence and covered their tracks; and then they complain to the mayor's office that we haven't found the killer yet."

"Can you prove that, lieutenant?"

"No sir. I can't prove it."

"Well, enough said about evidence tampering. Commander, give him more men. Let's close this case. What about the weapon, lieutenant?"

"The Medical Examiner recovered the .22-caliber slugs from the bodies. We searched the museum as thoroughly as we could, but there's no way we can take a place as big as that apart. I think we'll find the weapon when we find the shooter."

"If he still has it."

"My instincts tell me he's a pretty smug bastard. I think he'll still have it."

"What is this about their genitals being exposed?"

"They were wearing loincloths, chief. The killer twisted the loincloths to the side."

"What was the point of that?"

"I don't know, sir. Humiliation, I guess."

"Who would want to humiliate the corpses?"

"Goddamned pervert, if you ask me," Lloyd interjected.

"The media has been keeping the wires hot with your case, lieutenant. I need to see more progress than this.

Let's see if we can't kick this investigation into high gear. That's all for now."

Matt and Lloyd left the municipal building together.

"I want a meeting in my office first thing Monday morning, lieutenant. Make sure everyone connected with this investigation is at the meeting. I want to review everything you've found up to then . . . autopsy reports, interviews, everything," Lloyd insisted before he left.

"Fascist son of a bitch," Matt said to himself as he sat in his car brooding about the amount of overtime he had put in during the 10 years he had been on the force and how little he had gotten in return. He thought about time lost with Carla, his children, and his friends and family, time given up for his career. He usually managed to submerge his insecurity under a practiced facade of self-assurance. But today he felt the icy fingers of fear and uncertainty creeping back into his life, messing with his mind, making him question his future.

He began the drive to Fourth District headquarters when he made a sudden U-turn and headed home. When he arrived, he scooped up both children and headed back to the car. Carla followed them to the front porch.

"Where are you taking the children, Matthew?"

"To work with me."

"Please don't take them to work looking like that, honey. I haven't even combed Jenny's hair today."

"Her hair looks okay to me."

"Well, at least let me put some decent clothes on them."

"I don't have time for that, Carla."

"I don't want my children going on your job looking like bums, Matthew. People will think I'm an awful mother."

"Come with us, Mommy," Jenny called from the car.

"Come with us, Mommy," Robbie repeated.

"I wouldn't be caught dead in that car with the two of you looking like a couple of stray puppies."

Matt laughed, strapped the children into their seats, and drove off. The children laughed, too. They all waved good-bye to Carla.

CHAPTER 9

The next day, Matt called Sam Johnson's home number from his Fourth District office.

"Why are you pissing on my Sunday evening, Alexander? I already said I would be at the meeting tomorrow morning."

"I've been looking through the tests you've done so far, Sam, and they don't help me worth a damn. The only blood at the scene belongs to the victims. The blood spatter is inconclusive as to where the killer was standing or how far away he was. As a matter of fact, there's nothing in the report other than the bullets which show that a shooter was even at the scene."

"The same thing crossed my mind when I was writing up the report. Weird, ain't it?"

"Sam, I need a shooter. What about those latent prints you found at the scene?"

"They didn't match either victim. My only other alternative is to take elimination prints from all the staff in the museum, but what will that prove? Everybody in there will probably have a legitimate reason for being in that diorama at one time or another."

"You have got to cut me some slack, Sam. I need something to tie this case together, man. When are those tests going to be ready?"

"Not for several days. You know the drill, Alexander."

"I need something now, Sam."

"It ain't gonna happen, Alexander. Why you harping on my case, brother? You haven't even ID'd those bums yet."

"Don't remind me."

"What's the latest on the ID search, Alexander?"

"Pitiful. After you struck out on the AFIS, we blanketed the surrounding jurisdictions with their pictures and prints and not a peep so far. Lloyd and Chief Carter are in my shit, Sam. The secretary of the Smithsonian has pulled out all the stops trying to get this investigation wrapped up; and I don't even know who the damned victims are."

"You're in a tight spot, Alexander."

"Tell me something I don't already know, man."

"What did your professor up at Howard tell you?"

"He said the African costumes were Congolese and that the dust and grease were consistent with voodoo rituals."

Sam laughed out loud.

"You mean to tell me that those two jigaboos were working roots over at the Smithsonian?"

"That's what Dr. Phelps says."

"Well, ain't that a bitch? Looks like the voodoo didn't save their asses when the shooter came calling."

"Yeah, right. I'll see you at the meeting in the morning, Sam."

Matt left Fourth District Headquarters at eight

o'clock Sunday evening. Driving south on Georgia Avenue on his way home to LeDroit Park, he passed Lacy's Bar and Grill, his favorite watering hole, and decided to stop in for a drink. The Sunday crowd was still drifting in. Matt recognized many of the regulars who had given Bill Lacy a sizeable chunk of their monthly paychecks over the years. He wondered how they could afford to buy their drinks by the glass night after night when three or four nights a month at Lacy's prices would have put his budget way behind the eight ball and him in the dog house with Carla.

Matt didn't see any of his bullshitting buddies, so he went over to the bar and ordered a Maker's Mark on the rocks from Tiny Lacy, the club's bartender, superb cook, and brother of the owner. Tiny had retired early from one of the best restaurants in the District because his sizeable bulk had made it impossible for him to stand on his feet any longer. When Tiny left the Trade Winds, he went uptown to Brightwood to tend bar and cook in his brother's establishment. Tiny solved the problem of standing on his feet all day by using a reinforced swivel chair that all but disappeared under his enormous girth as he propelled it from one end of the glass-walled bar to the other to serve drinks and swap gossip which he devoured like a starving man on a deserted island.

"Long time no see, lieutenant," Tiny rasped with a throat that had seen far too much grill smoke.

"It's been a while, Tiny. How you been?"

"So-so, lieutenant. So-so. Where's your partner tonight?"

"Am I my partner's keeper, Tiny?"

Tiny laughed.

"No, sir. Jake don't need no keeper, that's for damn sure. He was just in here last night with his girlfriend, Yvonne," Tiny laughed. "No sir, old Jake don't need no keeper."

Matt laughs, too, amazed at how Jake continually managed to keep his wife Flo and his girlfriend Yvonne at a respectable distance from each other.

"You still keeping them criminals off the street, lieutenant?"

"Giving it my best shot, Tiny."

"Hey, Tiny! Bring your big fat ass down here and fix me another drink!" a drunk shouted from the other end of the bar.

"You just go right ahead and kiss my big fat ass, Leeroy. You'll get your next drink when I get good and damned ready to serve it, you flat-headed motherfucker."

Tiny tried to get angry, but he found himself laughing along with the other patrons at the bar.

"See there how he treats a paying customer," Leeroy complained to the other patrons. "I don't have to bring my trade to Lacy's, Tiny. I don't have to spend hard-earned money to be called a flat-headed motherfucker by a fat-assed son-of-a-bitch like you," Leeroy loudly protested as he got up and left the bar.

The other bar patrons laughed as Leeroy left.

"Look at him trying to act like he's leaving," Tiny complained. "He ain't going nowhere."

Matt turned to find Leeroy comfortably ensconced in

a booth with three women, placing a drink order with Sonja the waitress.

"Looks like you're right, Tiny," Matt says.

"I got that asshole's number," Tiny insisted. "He likes to ridicule and poke fun at people and then he tries to jump bad if you don't take his shit. Me and old Leeroy Williams go way back, and he's been a asshole the whole time I been knowing him."

"Hit me again, Tiny," Matt said.

"Sure thing, lieutenant."

"You ever hear of the Ife Temple, Tiny?"

"You talking about that place off Fourteenth Street where Kofi Asante supposed to be a high priest or something?"

"Yeah, that's it. How do you know Kofi Asante, man?"

"I been knowing him ever since he was a kid, lieutenant. You know his daddy's a doctor up on the Gold Coast. Kofi's one of the light brights trying to pretend he come from the ghetto. He was brought up in North Portal Estates where his mama and daddy still live."

"Is Kofi Asante his real name?"

"Heck no! His real name is Thomas Richard Terrell III. Doc Terrell's his daddy. He started calling himself Kofi Asante after he got real caught up in the black power movement when he was going to Howard back in the seventies, thought he was a revolutionary or something. Him and some other kids from Howard were arrested for trying to firebomb the South African embassy when he was 19. Kofi swears he didn't do it, but he was the only one who got convicted on that rap. Had to serve two years at Lorton. His family stuck by him, though, even while he was at Lorton. But after he got out, Kofi turned against his family. I hear he still don't have nothing to do with his own mama and daddy. He says they're too bougie for him and his crowd down at the Ife Temple. If it wasn't for his daddy, his butt would be sitting out on the street right now."

"How come you know him, Tiny?"

"Doc Terrell and my daddy grew up together in Baltimore. They still good friends."

"What do you know about the Ife Temple?"

"Temple, my ass. Doc Terrell bought that house for Kofi about 10 years ago. Kofi was renting the house, but he couldn't keep up the rent payments. Doc Terrell was driving by there one day and saw a for sale sign in the yard. He bought the house and lets Kofi live there. That's the only reason Kofi's got a roof over his head."

"How many people live there, Tiny?"

"Goo-gobs of Negroes, lieutenant. Doc Terrell is always paying to have the pipes fixed cause so many people live in that joint. It ain't nothing but a goddamned hippie commune. All the men got three or four wives and they got babies by all of them. I went to church over there once, but I didn't like it. Too much mishmash if you ask me. I asked Kofi why his service was so strange and he started telling me about all these rituals they practice, stuff from Ancient Egypt, Buddhism, and Judaism. Well, all them 'isms was more than I could take, so I didn't go back."

"Are any of the people at the Ife Temple legally married?"

"Is the Pope married? Heck, no, they ain't married. Kofi says it's against their religion to marry according to the white man's laws. They got their own marriage ceremony, and they can marry as many times as they want to. Every time my wife gets mad at me, I tell her I'm gonna join the Ife Temple and get me about five more wives. One of them's bound to like me just the way I am," Tiny laughed out loud.

"I was over there yesterday, Tiny. Most of the members look pretty young."

"They are young folk. There's not many old heads over there, just Kofi and a few others. I think they run the women off when they start getting some age on them. I ain't been over there in a long time, though."

"There was only one middle-aged woman in the entire service yesterday morning. She was tall and fair-skinned and looked like she was a priestess or something."

"That was Marian, Kofi's main wife. She still hanging in there, huh? I thought Kofi would've put her out to pasture by now because of her age. Looks like Marian's got staying power. Kofi color-struck, you know. He talks all that black power shit, but he don't like nothing but high yellow women with straight hair. Always has."

"What about Carlos Williams? You know him?"

"Yeah, I know that thug. Kofi met him at Lorton. They been ace-coon-boon buddies ever since. Kofi's parents hate Carlos' guts. They think Carlos is the reason Kofi turned on them; but I don't give Carlos that much credit. He wasn't nothing but a drug pusher and a enforcer before he got sent up. The word on the street is that Carlos will punch your lights for you if you know what I mean, lieutenant. Most people stay out of his way."

"What really goes on in the Ife Temple, Tiny?"

"I ain't never heard of nothing illegal happening over there, and that's the truth. I know they used to smoke a whole heap of marijuana and hashish. You could go over there and smoke it with them, but they wouldn't sell it to you; and you had to do work around the temple before they let you smoke. I ain't heard nothing about them smoking lately, though."

"What kind of people join the temple?"

"Drug users, kids out in the streets with no place to go, young kids been messed over by life who ain't got a job and no place to live. Kofi and Marian take them in and try to help them."

"What do they want from them?"

"They don't mess over kids, lieutenant. Marian never had any kids of her own so she tries to mother the kids who come there. Sometimes it works out, sometimes it don't; but they wouldn't do anything to hurt a young person."

"They marry them against the law, Tiny."

Tiny looked skeptical before he answered.

"Yeah well, you got a point there. I don't know how young those girls are when they get married at the Ife Temple. Can I get you a refill, lieutenant?"

"No thanks. Two is all I take when I'm driving," Matt

answered as Sonja the waitress walks over to his barstool.

"Well, well. If it isn't the almighty lieutenant Matthew Alexander."

"It's good to see you, too, Sonja."

"I am a sight for sore eyes, ain't I, sugar," Sonja said, standing very close to Matt with her back against the bar and her ample bosom displayed to its best advantage.

"Don't flatter yourself, Sonja. Compliments mean more when they come from someone else."

"Were you gonna compliment me, Lieutenant Alexander?"

"No I wasn't."

"That's why I toot my own horn, sugar. Give me three Jacks and two Johnnies on the rocks, Tiny," Sonja said as she turned around to the bar. "Tiny appreciates me, don't you, sugar?"

"You know I do, baby. You the finest thing I ever did see," Tiny replied, hanging over the bar in front of Sonja, practically drooling with a silly grin on his face.

"See there, lieutenant. Tiny knows a good woman when he sees one."

"Some people aren't as particular as they ought to be, Sonja."

"Hear that, Tiny? He says you aren't particular when it comes to women. That right?"

"Hell no! I don't mess with just anybody. You know that, Sonja. I like your style, baby," Tiny insisted, the silly grin still spread all over his face.

"Where my drinks, Tiny? I got customers waiting,

sugar."

"Coming up."

"So, how's the little family, lieutenant?"

"Couldn't be better, Sonja."

"Well ain't that just peachy," Sonja replied as she put the drinks on her tray. "Give me a ring when you get tired of playing house, sugar. I can make it worth your while," Sonja whispered to Matt before strutting away from the bar with her backfield in motion.

"That Sonja is something, ain't she, lieutenant?" Tiny asked with his eyes glued to Sonja's hips.

"If you like her type, Tiny."

"Sonja is the best waitress we ever had. She moves more liquor through this joint than the law allows. You wouldn't believe the tips she makes, man. Bill tried to get her to kick back some of her tips, but she raised so much hell he backed off. He didn't want her to quit. Half the men in here come to see Sonja."

Matt and Tiny watched as Sonja worked the crowd on her side of the bar. The other waitress, Jackie, tried to pander a watered-down version of Sonja's sex appeal on the other side of the room to little effect. It was clear that all the action was swirling around Sonja.

"I'm calling it a night, Tiny," Matt said as he got up to leave.

"Don't be a stranger, lieutenant. You always welcome at Lacy's."

Matt drove by the Ife Temple on his way home. The Eye of Ra was bathed in light from a street lamp at the corner of Fourteenth and Harvard, giving the impression the house never slept. Matt wondered whether either Kofi or Carlos had the skill to disable a multimillion dollar, state-of-the-art security system without tripping the alarms. He strongly doubted that they would have left the necklace behind if they had been involved in the theft. It was hard for him to imagine Kofi as a killer, but according to Tiny, Carlos fit the bill right down to the ground. Matt drove away from the Ife Temple with more questions than he had brought.

CHAPTER 10

"Have Mercy! I thought he'd never let up this morning. You'd think we shot those victims the way he was laying into us," Jake said after their eight o'clock meeting with Lloyd.

"He's pissed."

"What the hell does he expect us to do, pull the shooter out of thin air?"

"He's put two more detectives on the case. He told Bryant to spend more time on it, too."

"Who's going to keep Cullison informed behind our backs if Captain Bryant is working our investigation full time?"

"Henry Bryant can always find time to snitch."

"I know that's right," Jake agreed.

"I still can't believe we haven't ID'd the victims, Jake."

"Yeah, that's weird, man. They could have dropped in from outer space for all we know."

"Sam hung in there with Lloyd at the meeting, but Lloyd was right. How the hell are we gonna solve these homicides if we don't even know who the victims are?"

"Somebody knows who they are, man."

"Come on, Jake, Let's go."

"Where we going?" Jake asked as he followed Matt out of the office.

"To the Ife Temple."

"No more sermons, partner. I ain't listening to no more sermons."

Matt laughs. "A little preaching never hurt anyone, Jake, especially an old-time, foot-washing Baptist like you."

"I wouldn't mind listening if it was real preaching, but it ain't. It's just all that militant stuff, talking against the white man and the system. I fight the system all week; but when I go to church I don't want to hear nothing about the white man. I want to hear about the Lord."

After the two detectives waited in the alcove for several minutes, one of the sentries escorted them to Kofi's small private office behind the large assembly room.

"What do you want this time?" Kofi asked.

"Just a few more questions, Asante. When I questioned you at the museum, you said you bring the word of God to staff people at the Smithsonian."

"That's right, lieutenant. I will talk to anyone who is willing to listen to the word of the one true God."

"Have you made any converts at the Smithsonian?"

"I've gotten one or two people to come to the main service on Sunday, but none of them joined the temple."

"I need the names of anyone at the Smithsonian who's been to the Ife Temple."

"It's not against the law to worship at the Ife Temple, lieutenant. And this is still a free country."

"I still need the names, Asante. I also need the names of all the Ife Temple members who work at the

Smithsonian."

"Just Carlos and me, lieutenant. Nobody else works on that plantation."

"What kind of religion are you selling at the Ife Temple, Asante?"

"We're not selling religion, lieutenant. You can't sell spiritual enlightenment. It comes from a pure heart, a clean spirit, and total submission to the will of God."

Matt showed Kofi pictures of the murdered men.

"Do you recognize these men?"

"I told the policeman who showed me these pictures last Thursday that I didn't know these men. Why do you continue to take me over the same ground?"

"Somebody at the museum knew these men, Asante. That's the only way they could have gotten inside the building after hours. Since Jimmy Wilson overheard you and Carlos Johnson plotting to sneak unauthorized people into the museum after hours, you fit the bill to a 'T'."

"I didn't know them last Thursday and I still don't know them."

"If you don't know them, you won't mind if we show the pictures around the temple will you?"

"Why should I mind? I already told you that these men are strangers to the Ife Temple."

Matt and Jake spent the next hour showing the pictures to members of the temple. None of the temple faithful admitted knowing the murder victims. Matt tried hard to pump the members for more information about the temple, but everyone was close-mouthed. Matt was amazed at the number of people living in the large three-story house as he questioned over 30 people, excluding the children. The two detectives left the Ife Temple at twelve forty-five and drove over to the Medical Examiner's office at D.C. General Hospital.

"Why you going back to the morgue?"

"I need to talk to Steve Mitchell about the autopsies."

"He already sent the post-mortem report."

"I know he did, Jake."

They spent the better part of two hours talking to Steve Mitchell. Matt repeated Dr. Phelps' theory about the grease and ashes.

"That's priceless, Matt. Voodoo in the Smithsonian," Steve said, laughing.

"Yeah, I know what you mean. All that high-toned culture laid low by a couple of witch doctors."

"Have you seen today's paper? The Smithsonian is taking a real beating on those homicides, man. It's so bad Secretary Marshall had to go up on the Hill for a closed-door meeting with members of the House Appropriations Committee."

"Lloyd and Chief Carter have been tight in my shit ever since the homicides, man. They want this case closed, last week."

"I wish I could help you more, Matt. But aside from the grease and the ashes under the fingernails of the one victim, the homicides are pretty straightforward. The analysis of their stomach contents indicated that they hadn't eaten for several hours before they were killed. Looks like they had hamburgers late Tuesday afternoon; but they didn't eat anything after that. They didn't have any contusions, abrasions, or lacerations or any other wounds, for that matter. There was no sign of a struggle, no blood under either victim's fingernails. They were just shot to death. And believe me, I know all the signs of gunshot homicides. When you process nearly 200 homicides a year from gunshots, you can do the next one in your sleep, man, voodoo or no voodoo."

"What about their genitals being exposed the way they were?" Jake asked.

"I examined their genital areas closely, and they both looked normal to me. There were no marks on their penises or their scrotums. Other than that, I can't explain why their genitals were exposed."

"This case has got me going, Steve. When I told Lloyd that the Smithsonian has been covering its tracks since we started this homicide investigation, he accused me of crying wolf and gave me two more investigators to assist on the case. What case, I'd like to know?" Matt asked as he got up to leave. "Thanks for your time, Steve."

"I wish I had more to tell you, Matt," Steve replied as he walked them as far as the corridor outside his office. "How long do you want us to keep them on ice?"

"We're still trying to identify them. Give us some more time."

After they returned to Fourth District Headquarters, Matt stopped by the crime lab to talk to Sam, who was sitting behind his desk eating a late lunch.

"You look worried, Alexander."

"Why do you think we haven't been able to identify the victims, Sam?"

"Good question," Sam replied between bites. "I finally got a response from Immigration. They ran the victims' fingerprints against the database they keep on foreigners who've applied for permanent residency. The prints weren't in their database; but that doesn't mean they aren't African, because there are thousands of Africans in the country on student visas who aren't required to be fingerprinted. So where does that leave us?"

"Out in left field," Matt dejectedly replied before he sat down.

"What do you hear from the African embassies?" Sam asked.

"Two embassies have responded, and nobody ID'd the victims from the pictures we sent them."

"It don't look good."

"Tell me something I don't know, Sam."

"I've been thinking about your case, Alexander. Seems to me that what you got here are a couple of young black men who've never been in trouble with the law. Now what kind of young black men never get into trouble with the law?"

"I don't know what you mean?"

"Yes you do. Think about it. What kind of young black men never get into trouble with the law?"

"Smart, educated, from good families, wealthy. Shit, Sam. I don't know."

"No, you're right," Sam replied with his mouth full. "Think about your victims. Would you classify them as smart?"

"Hell no! They wouldn't be dead if they were smart."

"My point exactly. If they're not smart, or educated, or wealthy, and they haven't been in trouble with the law where did they come from?"

"You tell me, Sam."

"From the boonies. The way I see it you either got a couple of hicks or a couple of African students. Take your pick."

"What difference does it make? We still don't know who the hell they are?"

"The question you have to ask yourself lieutenant is, if they're hicks, what were they doing in those getups?"

"I've asked myself that question a hundred times, Sam."

"It's a very important question, lieutenant."

CHAPTER 11

"Hot damn! Did you read the Metro section of the *Post* this morning, Jake?"

"Yeah, I looked through it. So what?"

"So, did you read the article about the curator selling off jewels from the Smithsonian's gem collection without permission?"

"No, I passed on that one."

"Guess who that curator is, man."

"Don't have a clue, partner."

"Henry Hughes."

"Hughes?"

"Yeah. You remember Hughes, he's the one Jimmy Wilson said he told about Kofi Asante and Carlos Williams plotting to sneak someone into the museum after hours."

"Well, so what?"

"So, listen to what the article says: 'The Director of the Smithsonian's Museum of Natural History, William Fisher, has confirmed that a senior curator at the museum responsible for the Smithsonian's priceless gem collection is under investigation concerning the unauthorized sale of several items from the collection. The curator is suspected of selling jewels that had been donated to the Smithsonian with the explicit understanding that the jewels would not be de-accessioned and sold. The senior curator is also suspected of having sold other pieces of jewelry without the Smithsonian's permission."

"That's some bold shit, partner."

"Looks like there's more to Henry Hughes than meets the eye, Jake. Come on, man, let's go."

"Where to?"

"The Museum of Natural History, where else?"

When they arrived at the museum, Matt and Jake went directly to Fisher's office. Fisher's plump, middle-aged secretary remembered them; and before Matt could say a word, she jumped up from her desk and rushed into Fisher's office. When she returned she told them that her boss was in a meeting and that he would see them when the meeting was over. They waited five minutes, after which time Henry Hughes emerged from Fisher's office looking dazed and dejected. Hughes rushed out of Fisher's outer office before Matt could speak to him.

Fisher was not pleased to see the two detectives darken his door again.

"What can I do for you, Lieutenant Alexander?"

"What's this about Henry Hughes selling pieces from your gem collection without permission, Fisher?"

"Why is that any of your business?"

"I'm making it my business, Jack!" Matt angrily shouted. "I'm still investigating two unsolved murders and a major jewel heist from your gem collection."

"There's absolutely no connection between the

tumbled emerald necklace and Henry Hughes. Absolutely none."

"I'll be the judge of that, Fisher."

"What Henry Hughes did isn't the business of the District Police, lieutenant. The Smithsonian hasn't filed any charges against him, and we don't intend to. It's simply a question of mistaken judgment on his part."

"From where I stand, what Hughes did qualifies as a damned good motive for murder. Odds are that Hughes recruited the two murder victims to steal the necklace so he could sell it. I'm going after his ass, Fisher. You can't sweep this under the rug."

"If Henry had wanted to sell the emerald necklace, why did he leave it on the murder victims? Does that make any sense?"

"Not yet; but I've always suspected the victims had a connection inside the museum. Hughes put in a lot of overtime. He was working late the night the victims were killed, too. You knew Hughes was in the museum that night, Fisher, but you covered it up, just like you're trying to cover his tracks now."

"That's a damnable lie. I haven't covered up anything connected with those murders. As a matter of fact, I did everything I could to help you."

"Yeah, right, Fisher. Tell me anything."

"It's the truth. Why would I lie for Henry Hughes? I can't stand the man. He's caused more trouble for me than you'll ever know."

"What kind of trouble?" Matt asked.

"He has a personal vendetta against Andy Marshall.

Henry Hughes comes from a wealthy, well connected family in D.C. political circles.. He's on speaking terms with several influential congressmen whom he regularly feeds negative information about the Smithsonian. He's given me nothing but grief since I took this job six years ago."

"How long has Hughes been at the Smithsonian?"

"He's been here 12 years. He came shortly after Andrew Marshall was hired. He and Andy knew each other when they were undergraduates at Harvard. From what I understand, they worked together pretty well until Andy started moving up at ladder here and Hughes didn't. That's when the sabotage began."

"What kind of sabotage, Fisher?"

"Nothing that would make much sense to an outsider, lieutenant. I admit that Henry Hughes is damned spiteful; but he's not a murderer by any stretch of the imagination."

"That's your opinion, Fisher. The facts are that someone inside the Museum of Natural History who knew their way around the security alarms let the murder victims in here that Tuesday night. That same someone also knew enough to disable the security system for the gem collection. From where I sit, Henry Hughes is our man."

Matt and Jake headed for Hughes' office after they left Fisher's.

Matt knocked on Hughes' office door and entered without waiting for a reply. Henry Hughes was standing with his back to the door, staring out the one window in his office.

"Hughes, we need to talk."

Startled, Hughes turned and faced them.

"What are you doing in my office?"

"I knocked on the door."

"I didn't hear you knock, and I didn't tell you to come in. What do you want?"

"I want to talk to you about the murders."

"Good grief! Aren't you people ever going to let that drop? I told you when you were here before that I don't know anything about those murdered men."

"The murder victims stole a $10 million emerald necklace from your gem collection, Dr. Hughes. Today, I find out you've been selling jewels from the collection without permission. Even though you deny it, I know you were in the museum that Tuesday night when the victims were killed."

"That's a lie. I wasn't in the museum that night!" Hughes shouts at Matt.

"We can prove you were here, Hughes," Matt lied.

"It's a lie I tell you. I was home all evening."

"Can you prove that?"

"No, I can't prove it. I live alone."

"If you weren't in the museum, you shouldn't mind coming to Fourth District Headquarters with us and explaining exactly what you were doing when the homicide victims were killed."

"Are you arresting me?"

"No, I'm not arresting you; but I want you to make a formal statement about your whereabouts the night of the murders. You don't have to come with us if you don't want to. But, if you refuse, I will swear out a warrant for your arrest."

"Okay, I'll go with you. There's no point in staying here now that I've been fired," Hughes replied dejectedly.

"Fired. Since when?" Matt asked.

"Fisher fired me this morning. He gave me to the end of the week to clean out my office," Hughes explained as he locked his office door.

Matt mused over Hughes' firing on the way back to Fourth District Headquarters. Fisher had said that selling the jewelry was a mistake in judgment by Hughes, but it was clearly a lot more serious than that for the Smithsonian to have fired him. Hughes was silent during the ride to headquarters. After they arrived, Matt escorted Hughes to his second floor office.

"Why were you selling jewelry from the gem collection without permission?"

"See here, Lieutenant Alexander. As chief curator for the gem collection, I have authority to de-accession items from the collection to make room for pieces that fit into our collections policy better. Fisher knows that the pieces I de-accessioned were old and hadn't been displayed in decades."

"If that's true, why did Fisher fire you?"

"It's payback time, lieutenant. He fired me because I exposed their incompetence and corruption on the Hill. Andrew Marshall has been after me for years; and he finally found a way to destroy my career."

"How many pieces of jewelry did you sell?"

"Just five pieces; and none of them were significant."

"Who did you sell them to?"

"An antique jewelry collector."

"What antique jewelry collector, Hughes?"

"Herman Wittstein."

"What's his address?"

"I don't know it by heart; but he has a shop on Wisconsin and Canal in Georgetown."

"How much money did you get for the pieces?"

"Seven hundred and fifty thousand dollars, every penny of which I put back into my budget. It's all accounted for, and even Bill had to admit that I hadn't stolen any of the money."

"How do they know that's all the money you got from Herman Wittstein?"

"Because I gave Fisher the sale receipts for the jewelry. Bill got copies of the cancelled certified check from Wittstein's bank, too," Hughes earnestly explained.

Matt and Jake looked at each other.

"Cancelled checks don't mean anything when you're taking money under the table," Matt replied.

"That's a dirty lie. Fisher accused me of being on the take, too; but I didn't take a dime more than I sold the jewelry for."

"If that's true, why sell it on the 'QT' the way you did? Did you sell the pieces at market value?"

"I should have had them reappraised, but I went with the last appraised value we had."

"You said the jewelry hadn't been displayed in decades, so how long has it been since they were appraised?"

"I thought the last appraisal was recent, within the

past 10 years; but Bill said the pieces hadn't been appraised since 1970."

"A lot of water and money has passed under the bridge since the seventies, Hughes. So, how much money did you lose on the pieces?"

"They were worth three times more than I sold them for."

"Looks like Herman Wittstein hit the mother lode."

"Bill told me the Smithsonian is suing to recover the pieces from Wittstein."

"So, Hughes, how is it that you think you have the right to sell items from the gem collection when the Smithsonian says you don't."

"It's all a matter of interpretation, lieutenant."

"Yeah, right. I understand you work late a lot."

"I work late sometimes, but I didn't work late the night of the murders."

"Is it true that you never sign the log when you work late?"

"That's right. The logs are ridiculous."

"Your office is on the third floor near the gem exhibit, Hughes. Martha Darden said she saw a man on the third floor of the museum the night of the murders. If you were working late that night, it wouldn't have been hard for you to see or hear the victims in the gem exhibit."

"How many times do I have to tell you that I wasn't in the museum that night, lieutenant?"

"Everything is pointing in your direction, Hughes."

"That's merely your opinion, Lieutenant Alexander.

Where's the evidence you said you had against me?"

"I don't play my cards before I'm ready, Hughes. You'll know soon enough."

"It's all so ridiculous. I didn't know those men. What possible reason would I have had for killing them?"

"The emerald necklace."

"That's even more ridiculous. Why kill them for the necklace and leave it on the body?"

"You tell me."

"I told you I was home the night of the murders."

"Yeah, right. Those are all the questions I have for now, Hughes, but I'll be in touch. In the meantime, don't leave town," Matt warned Hughes as he left the office.

"He's a strange bird, all right," Jake admitted; "but he sure 'nough tore his ass when he sold that jewelry."

"I want a warrant to search his office, Jake. He seems sort of shell-shocked from being fired. If we hurry, we ought to be able to get in there before he cleans it out."

"Damn! I was on my way to get some lunch."

"There's nothing to stop you from getting lunch on your way back from Judge Parham's office."

"You coming with me?"

"It doesn't take two of us to get a warrant, man."

Jake grudgingly left Fourth District headquarters for the Judicial Building at the same time Fisher left the Museum of Natural History for a hastily called meeting with Secretary Marshall in the Castle.

"Jesus, Bill! It's getting to the point where I hate to see you coming. What is it now?"

"Lieutenant Alexander paid me a visit this morning,

Andy. He read about Henry in the paper; and he says the unauthorized sales make Henry a suspect in the homicides."

"Is he out of his mind? What has the sale of a few pieces of antique jewelry got to do with those murders?"

"He said the murders were an inside job. He swears that someone in the museum who knew how to disable the gem exhibit's security system let the murdered men into the museum the night they were killed."

"It's absurd to suspect Henry."

"That's how I feel, too, Andy; but given what Henry's been up to, I think we need to update our appraisals on the most valuable pieces in the collection. Since we already fired Henry, I'll have to bring someone in from the outside."

"How much is that going to cost us?"

"I have the money in my budget. Do I have your approval to go ahead with the appraisals?"

"Yes, you do. But keep it under wraps, Bill. I don't want this getting out."

"Okay. I'm worried about Henry, Andy. When I confronted him about selling that jewelry for one-third of what it was worth, he acted like it was no big deal. I can't figure him at all."

"He's not playing with a full deck, Bill. When we were at Harvard, the other fellows in our college thought he was an odd bird even then. I always defended him because he seemed to need a friend. He's an only child, you know. His parents are incredibly wealthy and very eccentric. Henry's getting to be just like them. He has a very lucrative trust fund, but you'd never know it from the way he lives. After he and Jean broke up, she had to haul him into court to get the alimony and child support he was ordered to pay her after their divorce settlement. He's very vindictive when he feels he's been wronged."

"I know it. He blames you for having him fired. Says you're paying him back for exposing how incompetent you are. I told him he was being fired for selling off the collection without permission, but he can't grasp the fact that his behavior is to blame for his situation."

"Typical. I can't tell you how relieved I am to finally be rid of Henry Hughes."

"I know what you mean; but I told Lieutenant Alexander that it's ridiculous to think that Henry would murder anybody. I don't believe he had anything to do with those murders."

"Neither do I."

"I gave him until Friday to clean out his desk. I'm having all the locks and the codes for the gem exhibit changed today. I'll serve as acting curator until I appoint an interim. I'll keep you informed about the results of the appraisal," Fisher said before leaving the secretary's office.

When Matt and Jake arrived at the museum with the search warrant, they found Willis Brandt getting ready to leave for the day. The look on his face made it clear they weren't welcome.

"What now, lieutenant?"

Matt handed him the warrant.

"Why do you want to search Henry Hughes' office?"

"Suspicion of two counts of first degree murder."

"First degree murder! Henry Hughes! You must be joking!"

"Do you see me laughing, Brandt?"

"I can't let you into Hughes' office without Kendricks' permission."

"Get his permission, then; but I'm not leaving here without searching that office."

Willis Brandt made a call to Col. Kendricks' office in the tower. They spoke only briefly before Brandt rang off.

"Kendricks is on his way over here."

Over at the Castle, Wallace Kendricks went straight from his office to the secretary's after speaking to Brandt.

"Sorry to barge in like this, Mr. Secretary, but I thought you needed to know that Lieutenant Alexander is over at Natural History right now with a warrant to search Henry Hughes' office."

"A warrant. What does he expect to find, Wally?"

"I don't know, sir. I'm on my way over there now."

"Lieutenant Alexander met with Fisher earlier this morning. He as much as accused Henry Hughes of murdering those men. I've never heard anything more outrageous."

"He must have something on Hughes."

"I'll be the first to admit that Henry Hughes is a pain in the ass; but he's not capable of murdering anyone. Lieutenant Alexander is barking up the wrong tree, Wally."

"He doesn't shoot from the hip, Mr. Secretary. I watched him closely while he was investigating the homicides back in June. He's very thorough and very deliberate. If he says that Hughes murdered those men, he's got something on him."

"He's also as stubborn as a mule, Wally. He accused Bill of covering up the fact that Henry was in the museum the night of the murders. I think Lieutenant Alexander is trying to make Henry a scapegoat for his unsolved murders. It's been two months since those men were killed, and the District Police still don't know who the victims are, let alone who the real killer is. It really galls me that he comes around stirring all this up again just when the incident has died down in the press."

"The fact of the matter is, we don't know who was in the museum the night of the murders, Mr. Secretary. Henry Hughes has a habit of working late, so he could very well have worked late that night."

"Henry says he wasn't in the museum, Wally. Why shouldn't we believe him?"

"I'm not saying we shouldn't, sir, but Lieutenant Alexander is a straight shooter. He wouldn't accuse Hughes of murder on a whim."

Kendricks rushed over to Brandt's office after his meeting with Secretary Marshall. After reading the warrant, Both Kendricks and Brandt escorted Matt and Jake to Henry Hughes' third-floor office.

"Is Hughes still in the museum?" Matt asked.

"No he isn't," Brandt replied. "His secretary told me he left early this afternoon and didn't come back to the office."

"What are you looking for?" Kendricks asked Matt.

"Something to connect Hughes to the homicides,"

Matt replied as he began searching through Hughes' desk.

They searched the office thoroughly, finding nothing incriminating. Wallace Kendricks agreed to let them search Hughes' laboratory, where they again come up empty handed. When they left the Museum of Natural History at seven-thirty that evening, they passed Henry Hughes as he was coming into the museum. He acted as if he didn't see them. They continued on to their car.

"It's a good thing we finished searching his office before he got back, partner."

"Yeah, right. I wonder why he's showing up for work at this hour?"

"Who knows. That dude is weird, man. Where to, Matt?"

"Home, James."

"Who you calling James?."

"Your name is James, isn't it?"

"That's my name, but I ain't your damned chauffeur."

"Yeah, right," Matt laughed. "I'll be in late tomorrow, man. I'm going over to Georgetown to talk to Herman Wittstein about that jewelry he bought from Dr. Hughes."

CHAPTER 12

The following Tuesday morning, Matt arrived at Wittstein Jewelers in Georgetown just as Herman Wittstein was rolling up the metal window guards outside his shop. Wittstein continued what he was doing as Matt introduced himself. The jewel merchant gave Matt a skeptical look before entering his elegant shop. Matt followed him inside.

"You're from the District Police. So what have I done, Lieutenant Alexander?"

"The Smithsonian is suing you to recover the jewelry you bought from Henry Hughes. You tell me what you've done, Mr. Wittstein."

"I'll see their asses in court!" Wittstein angrily shouted. "I bought those jewels fair and square, and I'll fight all the way to the Supreme Court to keep them! Why'd they let Henry Hughes sell the damned jewels, if they wanted to keep them in their collection?"

"Hughes sold the jewelry without the Smithsonian's permission, Mr. Wittstein. That makes the jewelry stolen merchandise, so the Smithsonian has a right to reclaim it."

"Over my dead body will they get them back! I've got the best lawyers in the District! They get nothing back from me! Nothing!" Wittstein shouted as he pounds his fist on the glass countertop. "I paid $750,000 for those jewels; and I have the bill of sale from the Smithsonian to prove it."

"The sign outside says you're an appraiser, Mr. Wittstein, so you must have known that you were buying that jewelry for one-third of its market value."

Herman Wittstein gave Matt a knowing look.

"I'm not an expert on antique jewelry, lieutenant. Henry Hughes said the Smithsonian had already appraised the jewelry and who am I to argue with the Smithsonian's appraised value?" he cunningly replied.

"Especially if their appraised value is just one-third of what you can sell the jewelry for."

"Let the seller beware. Is it my fault they hadn't had the jewels appraised in twenty years?"

"That's just what I want to talk to you about, Mr. Wittstein; how did you manage to swing such a sweetheart deal with Hughes?"

"It was no sweetheart deal, lieutenant. I paid seven hundred fifty thousand of my hard-earned dollars for those jewels."

"Henry Hughes was fired from the Smithsonian yesterday because they think he took money under the table to sell you the jewels cheap."

"It's a filthy, disgusting lie!" Wittstein shouted.

Matt backed up from the glass countertop, which Wittstein continued to pound with his fist.

"Look at it from the Smithsonian's point of view, Mr. Wittstein. Henry Hughes sells you the jewelry for one third of what it's worth without permission. You have to see that he put himself way out on a limb. Now, why would he do that? The most obvious reason is that there was something in it for him, something like a bribe from you."

"You can't prove I did anything illegal," Wittstein insisted with a very anxious look on his face.

"I wouldn't be so sure of that, Wittstein. Henry Hughes has been fired. The Smithsonian doesn't have to shield him anymore, so they're going to throw the book at you to recover the jewelry."

"I've got the best lawyers that money can buy, the best!"

"There's more than jewelry at stake here, Wittstein. Henry Hughes is suspected of murder in connection with the two homicides in the Museum of Natural History back in June."

"Murder! What have those murders got to do with Henry Hughes selling me the jewels?"

"You tell me, Mr. Wittstein."

"I don't know a damned thing about those murders! Not a damned thing!"

"Have it your own way, Wittstein, but if we take Henry Hughes down for two counts of murder one, anyone involved is going down with him," Matt warned before leaving the shop.

Herman Wittstein watched Matt's departure from behind the jewelry-filled glass countertop where he was standing. His anxiety-ridden face showed his age and the cost of the struggle he had waged to keep his business going over the previous 40 years. His thoughts drifted to his two sons, who for the past five years, had been after him to retire. Until he met Lieutenant Matthew Alexander that Tuesday morning, he had refused to take his sons' advice seriously.

The following Friday, Matt decided to pick Henry Hughes up for further questioning. When he and Jake arrived at the Museum of Natural History at 11 o'clock, Hughes' young secretary informed them that he hadn't been back to work since Monday; and that she hadn't been able to reach him at his Georgetown condominium. She also told them that Henry Hughes' staff was worried about him; and that they had met with Fisher earlier that morning to voice their concerns. Matt and Jake left Hughes' office and went downstairs to Willis Brandt's office.

"What is this about Hughes being missing, Brandt?"

"Who says he's missing?"

"His secretary said he hasn't been back to work since Monday and that she can't reach him at his apartment."

"Fisher fired Henry Hughes on Monday. I figured he got mad and just took off. I don't know anything about him being missing."

"Has he called in since Monday?" Matt asks.

"No, he hasn't called the museum. Fisher called me this morning and asked me to check around to see if he had called anybody on campus."

"Who's his next of kin?"

"His ex-wife, Jean Hughes. She lives in Arlington."

"Have you called her?"

"No, but I was going to call her today, since Hughes still hasn't cleaned out his office."

"I need to get back into Hughes' office, Brandt"

"For what?"

"I don't have to tell you that. The search warrant is still in force."

"Yeah, well you'll have to wait until I finish what I was doing!" Brandt angrily replied.

"We'll wait right here, Jack!" Matt answered just as angrily.

Brandt soon finished his paperwork and escorted them upstairs to Henry Hughes' office. After searching through Hughes' files for over an hour, Matt pulled three file folders and left.

"Where to next, man?"

"Jean Hughes' house in Arlington. Here's the address."

They arrived in front of an impressive three-story brick colonial in an exclusive Arlington neighborhood at two o'clock. They sat in the car and finished their hamburgers.

"Have mercy! That is a serious house. They must pay damned good money at the Smithsonian?"

"Henry Hughes didn't buy this house on his salary from the Smithsonian, man. He's rich."

"No shit! A rich weirdo."

"Just for the record, Jake. When you're rich and strange you're called eccentric."

They finished their carryout lunch in the car, after which Jake followed Matt up the winding walkway to the front of the house. An elderly couple walking their dog in front of the house stared at the two black detectives belligerently. Matt and Jake ignored them and their viciously barking dog. Matt rang the doorbell several times. A middle-aged white woman in pants and a pullover opened the door.

"Mrs. Hughes?"

"No sir. I'm Mrs. Phillips, the housekeeper. Mrs. Hughes went over to the school to pick her children up."

Matt showed Mrs. Phillips his badge.

"I'm Detective Lieutenant Matthew Alexander, Mrs. Phillips. I need to ask Mrs. Hughes some questions about her husband. May we come in and wait for her?"

"Well, sir, I don't know about letting you in while she ain't home. She'll be back directly," Mrs. Phillips replied, as she left the door cracked and stepped out onto the porch.

"When was the last time you saw Henry Hughes, Mrs. Phillips?"

"I haven't seen him in quite a while, lieutenant. Since they divorced last year, I hardly see him at all."

"So, you haven't seen him this week?"

"No, sir. I keep house for Mrs. Hughes during the week. I understand he comes over to see the children on weekends, but I'm not here then."

"How did Henry and Jean Hughes get along, Mrs. Phillips?"

"A whole lot better since they divorced. Mr. Hughes was a hard man to live with. I'm not one to spread gossip," Mrs. Phillips continued with little reservation, "but he was a strange one, Henry Hughes. Argued with his wife about everything, especially money. He didn't want her to spend an extra penny if he hadn't approved it beforehand. Kept her on a tight lead until she got tired of his peculiar ways and filed for divorce. She tried to get some of that trust fund of his, but his lawyers wouldn't let her have a penny. All she gets is child support and alimony, and he's behind on that this month."

"When does she get her support payment from Henry Hughes?"

"It's supposed to come by the fifteenth of every month, but it ain't come this month. I don't know how she's going to pay me if it don't come. She don't have a penny of her own."

"Has Mrs. Hughs mentioned anything about not being able to reach him this week?"

"Well sir, she did mention that she had tried to get in touch with him Wednesday night to see if he had mailed her money, but there was no answer. She figured he was traveling out of town for his job. Here she comes, now," Mrs. Phillips said as a champagne-colored Jeep Grand Cherokee pulled into the driveway. The children jumped out of the car and headed toward the front porch, where Matt and Jake were standing with Mrs. Phillips. Mrs. Hughes called them back and the three of them went into the house through the garage. Mrs. Phillips let Matt and Jake inside the house. Then she went back into the kitchen where Mrs. Hughes and the children were.

"Why do you want to know where Henry is?" Jean Hughes demanded as she walked across the living room into the foyer where Matt and Jake were standing.

"He hasn't been to work since Monday, Mrs. Hughes."

"Why is that a police matter? Henry travels all the time."

"He's not traveling on Smithsonian business."

"How do you know that?"

"Because he was fired from the Smithsonian last Monday morning."

"Fired from his job! I don't believe you!" Jean Hughes said as she nervously backed into her living room and sat down.

"Call William Fisher, Mrs. Hughes. He's the one who fired your ex-husband."

"Why was he fired?"

"You'll have to ask Fisher about that. Your ex-husband's secretary told me she had been trying to reach him since Wednesday. She said he wasn't answering the telephone at his apartment. When was the last time you spoke to him?"

"Let me think. It was last Saturday. He came over to pick the children up Saturday morning. He took them to the zoo, and he brought them home later that evening. That's the last time I spoke to him. I called him this past Wednesday night, but he didn't answer."

"Did he mention anything about going out of town when you saw him on Saturday?"

"No, he didn't."

"Would he leave town without telling you, Mrs. Hughes?"

Jean Hughes hesitated before answering.

"Yes he would, lieutenant. He's incredibly insensitive."

"Does he have other relatives in the area?"
"No. No relatives and almost no friends."
"Do you have any idea where he could be?"
"I'll call his parents to see if he's been in touch with them."

When Jean Hughes returned she informed Matt that Henry Hughes' parents hadn't heard from him in two weeks.

"Does he have a girlfriend?"
"I have no idea, Lieutenant Alexander."
"We're going to run by his place when we leave here, Mrs. Hughes. If you hear from him, please give me a call at Fourth District Headquarters at this number," Matt said as he handed Jean Hughes one of his cards.

They left Arlington and headed for Henry Hughes' Georgetown condominium. The superintendent of Hughes' building, Roger Frankel, was adamant about not letting them into the apartment until Matt told him that Hughes had been missing since Monday. Then Frankel remembered that he hadn't seen Henry Hughes leaving for work during the past week. Frankel also voiced concern about the accumulation of mail in Hughes' mailbox before he reluctantly took Matt and Jake up to the fifth-floor apartment. As he opened the door to 537 he sniffed the air expectantly then let the two detectives go in first.

Matt was surprised by the spartan, utilitarian furnishings they found in the three-bedroom apartment. He checked the bathroom to see if Hughes' toilet items were still there. They were. Matt also found a prescription bottle with pills for hypertension. He noted the doctor and the pharmacy. Then he checked the closet for luggage and found a full set, including a garment bag. He was convinced that Henry Hughes had not left his apartment willingly. After Matt and Jake walked through the apartment without finding a body, Frankel abandoned his position in front of the door and started looking around, too.

"Can you believe this place? How anybody with as much money as Henry Hughes can live like this is beyond me," Frankel said.

"How do you know how much money he has?" Matt asked as he and Jake began to search more systematically for clues to Hughes' disappearance.

"It may not look like it from the outside, but this is a very exclusive condominium, lieutenant. You have to have a net worth way up in seven figures to buy an apartment in this building. Believe me, the condominium association scrutinized Henry Hughes' net worth down to the last penny. He's worth a bundle. Matter of fact, he can buy and sell anybody in this building with plenty to spare, and this is how he chooses to live."

"Looks like money don't mean much to Hughes," said Jake.

"It may mean too much," Matt replied. "Maybe that's why he doesn't want to spend it. When was the last time you saw Henry Hughes, Mr. Frankel?"

"Monday morning around seven o'clock. I usually speak to him as he leaves for work."

"Are you certain you haven't seen him since then?"

"I have a good memory, Lieutenant Alexander. I

haven't seen him since Monday."

"Does he have any friends in the building?"

"No. When he moved in last year, several of the single ladies tried to cozy up to him because of his money, but he wasn't interested. He's a loner. Doesn't have one friend in the building that I know of."

"Does he get many visitors?"

"No. He's lived here over a year, and the only people I've seen visit him are his children."

"Thanks for letting us in the apartment, Mr. Frankel. Here's my card. Call me if you hear anything from Henry Hughes."

They arrived back at headquarters at four-thirty. Matt checked his voice mail and found a call from Bill Fisher. He returned the call.

"Have you found Henry Hughes?" Fisher asked.

"No we didn't find him. We've filed a missing person's report on him."

"Henry is doing this out of spite, lieutenant. He's a vindictive man. He's hiding out somewhere to make us look bad."

"That's your theory, Fisher. He hasn't mailed his support payment to his wife this month, so my theory is that he really is missing. Either way, it doesn't look good."

"You're the one who put all that pressure on him, accusing him of murder. I told you Henry wasn't capable of murder. It's your fault if he's done away with himself."

"You were the one who fired him, Fisher. If you need to blame someone, blame yourself," Matt angrily replied before hanging up in Bill Fisher's face.

CHAPTER 13

The DCPD made little progress in discovering Henry Hughes' whereabouts over the next several days. When Matt called Jean Hughes the following Wednesday, he discovered she still hadn't heard from Hughes or received her support check. She informed Matt that she had contacted her ex-husband's lawyer about the missing check. Matt got the lawyer's address from Jean Hughes and paid him a visit. He learned very little about Henry Hughes' finances and nothing at all that would explain where Henry Hughes was. Matt was very concerned because Hughes had been the most promising lead so far in solving the Smithsonian homicides.

Three days earlier, Fisher had met with Daniel Rhinehart, a private gem appraiser, to explain the need to begin updating the museum's older appraisals on the gem collection, starting with the best pieces. He also explained the security protocol he had established for Rhinehart while he was at the Smithsonian. Rhinehart had been put to work on the collection in Henry Hughes' laboratory the same day he was hired. The following Wednesday after he started work, Rhinehart requested a meeting with Fisher, Wallace Kendricks, and Willis Brandt at three in the afternoon.

When Fisher, Kendricks, and Brandt arrived for the meeting they found Rhinehart completing his appraisal of the tumbled emerald necklace. After he finished the examination, he meticulously cleaned and replaced all of the equipment he had used. Fisher became annoyed waiting for Rhinehart to get to the point of the meeting.

"What can you tell me about this emerald necklace?" Rhinehart asks Fisher.

"It's priceless, one of our best pieces. Why do you ask?"

"Why do I ask? I ask because it's a superbly rendered, expertly crafted fake."

"Goddammit, man! What do you mean it's a fake?!" Fisher shouted, snatching the necklace from the table in front of Rhinehart to inspect it more closely.

"I mean just what I said, Mr. Fisher. It's an exquisite reproduction, but still a fake. The diamonds are genuine; but it's worth no more than $10 thousand."

Fisher looked like a man whose life hung by a thread. He turned white as a sheet as the color drained from his face while he let the necklace slip from his grip back to the surface of the table.

"It can't be a fake."

"I tell you it *is* a fake. I examined it thoroughly several times."

"You need to sit down, man," Kendricks advised Fisher.

Fisher groped for a chair near the table as he continued to stare at the fake emeralds in front of him.

"I think we ought to check the necklace in the exhibit, too," Kendricks quietly suggested.

"I'll bet that's where the genuine necklace is," Fisher

desperately replied. "We must have gotten them mixed up somehow."

" We can't make any assumptions until Rhinehart looks at that one, too," Kendricks insisted.

"Is there another necklace?" Rhinehart asked.

"It's a long story," Kendricks answered; "but, yes, there is another emerald necklace identical to this one on display in the gem exhibit. You know the new codes, don't you, Fisher?"

"Yes, I know them."

Kendricks, Brandt, and Fisher retrieved the second necklace. Daniel Rhinehart examined the second necklace as meticulously as he had examined the first. The tension in the air was palpable as Rhinehart finished his examination.

"This is a fake, too."

Fisher staggered over to a chair and collapsed. He was visibly shaken when Daniel Rhinehart handed him the second necklace.

"This necklace is as superbly crafted as the one you're holding, Mr. Fisher. Whoever made these necklaces is a master craftsman. Not many people around who can do work like this anymore."

"Who would you go to if you wanted to have reproductions like these made?" Kendricks asked Rhinehart.

I can think of only two people offhand, and they both work in the New York diamond district. I'll give you their names."

"How can they both be fakes?" Fisher asked no one in particular. "And where in God's name is the genuine necklace?"

"It's obvious that Henry Hughes has stolen the real necklace, Fisher. That's why he's disappeared. There's no telling where that necklace is by now," Kendricks replied.

"It takes time to make reproductions of this quality. Whoever ordered them planned the theft months in advance," Rhinehart insisted.

"How far in advance, Mr. Rhinehart?" Kendricks asked.

"I'd say a conservative estimate is six months to a year."

Fifteen minutes later, they were all seated in Andrew Marshall's office with the two fake necklaces on the secretary's desk. Andrew Marshall looked grim as Daniel Rinehart reported on the outcome of his appraisals and left the meeting.

"This is a nightmare, Bill. Where the hell is the genuine necklace?"

"The only person who can answer that is Henry Hughes, Andy."

"Do you realize how bad this makes us look, Bill? All hell will break loose when the press finds out that Henry Hughes has disappeared with a priceless emerald necklace."

Fisher sat slumped in his chair.

"I know how it looks, Andy. Rhinehart said the fakes are so good, it took months to make them. So Henry must have been planning the theft for months."

"Damn it to hell, Bill. I thought you ran a tight ship in Natural History. What am I supposed to tell the board when they ask me what is going on in your shop? Two murders and the theft of a $10 million necklace."

"I know it looks bad, Andy, but I do my job. You know I do my job."

"What do you have to say for yourself, Wally? We've put a fortune into the security systems in Natural History, and for what I'd like to know when we have thieves, murderers, and priceless necklaces walking in and out of the place like an open-air market. What the hell is going on in your shop, Wally?"

"I can't tell you anymore than I already have, sir."

"Can either one of you explain why I shouldn't fire both of you right now?" Andrew Marshall shouted. "Do you have any idea how much hot water I'm in?"

Neither Fisher or Kendricks replied.

"This is the worst mess I've had to deal with in my 15 years at the Smithsonian. The absolute worst. I may not be able to ride this one out. But I'm telling both of you right here and now, if I go down, you're going with me."

Fisher slumped lower in his seat. Kendricks got a pained look on his downcast face. Willis Brandt sat rigidly still.

"What the hell do you suggest we do about the missing necklace, Bill?"

"I don't know what to tell you, Andy. We still don't know where Henry Hughes is."

"What do you suggest, Wally?"

"I think we ought to sit tight for the time being, Mr. Secretary. Nobody knows that the necklace found on the murder victim is a fake but us and the appraiser. Fisher says Rhinehart is discreet; so I think that buys us enough time to find Henry Hughes. The District Police have filed a missing persons report on him. They haven't come up with anything, yet; but they're looking for him."

"So what if we do find him and he's sold the damned necklace? Where does that leave us?"

"Up a creek," Kendricks replied.

"If Hughes were here right now, I could easily murder him with my bare hands," Fisher insisted.

Secretary Marshall gave Fisher a look of pure disgust.

"We have to notify the insurance company about the theft soon, Andy. Henry stole the necklace two months ago, so he's probably sold it by now," Fisher insisted.

"Even if he has sold it, we have nothing to lose by waiting a week or two to see if the District Police manage to run Henry Hughes to ground. I think we should keep everything under wraps for now," Kendricks insisted.

Secretary Marshall reluctantly agreed to go along with Kendricks' recommendation. The meeting adjourned. Fisher was totally dejected as he left the secretary's office. Willis Brandt and Kendricks conferred for several minutes in the corridor outside the secretary's suite of offices, after which Brandt returned to the Museum of Natural History. He rounded up Earl Simms and one other security guard whom he trusted. The three of them went up to Henry Hughes' office on the third floor of the museum. They began an exhaustive search of his office and laboratory for the real necklace. They searched for the remainder of the day without any success.

The following Friday morning, Matt was sitting in his office when his telephone rang.

"What can I do for you, Simms?"

"You remember that list I made out for you about who was at the crime scene right after I found the bodies, lieutenant?"

"Yes, I still have the list."

"Well, I just remembered somebody I left off the list. Kofi Asante."

"Kofi Asante was in the museum that Wednesday morning? I thought he worked the second-shift."

"He does work second-shift. When I asked him what he was doing there so early, he told me he had brought some relatives from out of town to visit the museum."

"That's all very interesting, Simms. Is that all he said?"

"Yeah. That's all. Have you found any trace of Hughes yet, Lieutenant Alexander?"

"Not yet, Simms, but we're still looking for him."

"It's kinda strange that he would up and disappear like that."

"Yeah, I know what you mean."

"We didn't find anything when we searched his office the other day."

"Why were you searching his office, Simms?"

"We were looking for the emerald necklace. Chief Brandt said it's missing."

"The hell it is! I told Kendricks and Brandt they had to keep that necklace safe. How long has it been missing?"

"Chief Brandt asked me and Watkins to help him look for the necklace on Wednesday."

"So, its been gone for two days?"

"I guess so, lieutenant, but I can't say for sure. Don't mention my name when you talk to Chief Brandt. He would make my life miserable if he found out I been spilling the beans to the DCPD."

"I won't mention you, Simms."

Matt waited for Jake to come in before they left for the Museum of Natural History. Matt decided to tackle Willis Brandt first.

"Christ! What is it now, lieutenant?"

"I hear that the number one piece of evidence in this case is missing, Brandt."

"I don't know what you're talking about."

"Hey, man. If you're trying to blow more smoke up my ass, it's not working. That emerald necklace is missing and I want to know what the happened to it."

"It's none of your business what happened to it."

"Listen up, asshole. I told Secretary Marshall that necklace had to be kept under tight security; and he promised that nothing would happen to it. Now the necklace is missing and I want to know what the hell happened."

"Shows how much you know, lieutenant. Nothing happened to the freaking necklace. It's still in the vault where we put it two months ago; but guess what asshole, it's a fake, too"

"That's a lie. I saw Henry Hughes appraise that necklace. He said it was genuine."

"He lied. It's as fake as the necklace left in the case."

"How long have you known it's a fake, Brandt?"

"I don't have anything else to say."

Matt and Jake paid a visit to Kendricks in the castle. Kendricks reluctantly agreed to meet with them.

"Why didn't you inform us that the necklace we found on the murder victim is a fake, Kendricks?"

"We didn't find out ourselves until this past Wednesday."

"That necklace is material evidence in a double homicide case. We have a right to know whether it's genuine or not."

"We thought the necklace was genuine just like you did. The only reason we had it reappraised at all is that Hughes got caught red-handed selling the other pieces from the collection without permission. Hughes fooled everybody."

"Two fake necklaces. You know what that means, Kendricks? It means that Hughes planted both necklaces."

"The thought did occur to me, lieutenant."

"If the homicide victims didn't steal the genuine necklace, what were they doing in the museum?"

"I don't know what they were doing besides getting themselves killed. It's obvious that Henry Hughes is the mastermind behind the theft."

"You should have informed me that the necklace we found is a fake, Kendricks."

"We were trying to wait until you found Henry Hughes. We wanted to hear what he had to say before we reported anything. Hughes may still have the genuine emerald necklace."

"Give me a break, Kendricks. Hughes stole that necklace two months ago. You know damned well he's sold it by now."

"I don't know what he's done with it; but I wanted to give him a chance to explain. There's a lot riding on where that necklace is, and the secretary wants to recover it without a lot of ugly publicity."

"We kept the theft out of the press the last time around, Kendricks. I'm not covering for you this time."

"All we're asking for is a week, Alexander. We'll have to go public with the theft ourselves after that."

"You've got a lot of nerve asking me for anything."

"All I'm asking is that you hold off until Hughes shows up again."

"I wouldn't count on seeing Henry Hughes again, Kendricks."

After Matt and Jake left the Smithsonian, they drove uptown to the Ife Temple where Matt demanded to see Kofi Asante.

"Why didn't you tell us you were in the museum Wednesday morning after the murders, Asante?"

"I didn't tell you because you didn't ask me."

"That's a lie. You told us you were at home."

"I was at home, lieutenant. I didn't go to the museum until after 11 o'clock Wednesday morning."

"Why so early? You don't report for work until five o'clock."

"I had some people visiting from out of town who wanted to see the museum."

"Who were the people?"

"Just some friends from out of town. What does it matter who they were?"

"You told Earl Simms they were relatives from out of town."

"I told Simms they were friends from out of town just like I'm telling you."

"Who are they and where're they from?" Matt demands.

"Mitch and Rosalind Thomas from Greensboro, North Carolina."

"I want their address and telephone number, now."

"Yeah, well you'll have to wait until I get it from my office."

"I'll go back there with you," Matt said as they followed Kofi back to his office.

Matt used Kofi's telephone to make a credit card call to the number Kofi gave him in Greensboro. He hung up after an answering machine picked up on the other end. Kofi looked as if he'd gotten a reprieve.

"What's the matter, lieutenant? You think I'm lying?"

"I know you're lying," Matt replied as he and Jake left the Ife Temple.

"Where to?" Jake asked.

"To Judge Parham's to get a warrant to search Hughes' apartment."

When they arrived at Hughes' condominium with the warrant later that afternoon, Roger Frankel bombarded them with questions about Henry Hughes' disappearance. He was still asking questions as he took them up to the apartment.

"We still haven't found him, Mr. Frankel."

"I can't understand why he didn't tell me what his travel plans were, lieutenant. I've been collecting his newspapers and mail, but who knows when he'll be back?"

Frankel left them in the apartment and went back downstairs. Matt went into Hughes' study and started searching through the papers on top of his desk. Jake began looking through the four-drawer file cabinet.

"What are we looking for, man?"

"Invoices, letters, sales slips, anything that shows Hughes bought those fake necklaces or sold the real emerald necklace. He'd have to be a fool to keep incriminating evidence like that, but who knows. He may have thought he was too smart to be caught."

They spent the better part of the afternoon sorting through papers they found in the apartment without finding what they were looking for.

"Looks like he covered his tracks pretty good, Matt."

"Yeah, right."

Matt looked behind all the pictures and paintings on the walls.

"You looking for a safe?"

"Yeah, but it looks like we're out of luck," he replied as he looked under the inexpensive rugs that covered most of the hardwood floors.

"Bingo, Jake. I found it," Matt called from the children's room. "It's near the head of this twin bed. Help me move it."

They moved the bed and the rug to reveal a small safe

under an expertly camouflaged hinged door that sat flush into the wooden floor. Matt pressed what looked like a knot in the wooden door and it flew open, exposing a combination lock.

"Damn, Jake. Looks like we hit the wall. There's no way we can open this safe."

Jake looked over Matt's shoulder.

"Have mercy! That's a serious piece of work."

"Who do you know on the outside that can crack it for us, man?"

"Roscoe's still in the slammer. Willie T.'s got arthritis so bad, he's had to give up stealing. He's preaching and passing the cup down on Fourteenth and Georgia, " Jake laughed. "The only person I know who might be able to crack it is Skinny Lester."

"Skinny's the worst crackhead in the District, man. How's he gonna open a safe like this?"

"Safe cracking is second nature to Skinny, man, whether he's stoned or not."

"You think you can find him?"

"Yeah, I know where he hangs out down on Florida Avenue."

"Go pick him up. I'll wait here until you get back."

An hour later, Jake returned with Skinny Lester, who started casing the apartment as soon as he walked through the door. Skinny's short, rail thin body barely supported a pair of out-sized blue jeans that sagged dangerously around his hips. He wore a big retro afro over an oversized pair of dark glasses that covered a good part of his emaciated face. Skinny carried a filthy white athletic bag in one hand as he walked around the apartment sizing up the merchandise.

"Damn! Ain't shit in here worth stealing, man," Skinny insisted, his eyes darting around the apartment as he wiped his runny nose with the sleeve of his shirt.

"I didn't bring you over here to steal, fool. We got a job for you."

"How much you paying?"

"Who said we was paying you anything?"

"I don't work for nothing, man. You know me better than that."

"There might be something in it for you if you crack the safe. You don't get shit if you can't open it," Jake promised.

"There ain't been a safe made I can't crack. Where is it?"

"It's through here," Matt said as he led Skinny to the safe.

"Watch out now! A Ferguson! It's been a long time since I saw something as beautiful as this."

Skinny smiled as he sat on the floor beside the safe and took his tools out of the bag.

"A Ferguson. The finest safe I ever cracked. It's a pleasure to do business with you, gentlemen, a pleasure."

Skinny pulled a stethoscope from his bag. He placed it against the safe and twirled the locking mechanism around several times. He kept up a steady stream of conversation as he listened to the safe as intently as a cardiologist listening to a sick heart.

"I was born to crack safes. Some people are born to dance, some are born to sing, preach, cook, fix cars; but I was born to crack safes. People don't believe me when I tell them it's a gift from God. They say why would God give somebody a gift to do something illegal like safe cracking? I don't know why. All I know is that safecracking is my gift. There's nothing gives me more pleasure."

"What about all that dope you shoot up, Skinny?"

"Dope ain't pleasure, man. It's agony. I shoot up because I'm a junkie. I can't help being a junkie anymore than I can help cracking safes."

"You saying God made you a junkie, too?"

"Naw, I can't blame that on the Lord. But I take the bitter with the sweet, sergeant. You can't have day without night just like you can't have heat without cold. There's two sides to everything. The Chinese call it Yin and Yang. I'm a safe cracker and a junkie. That's who Skinny Lester is. I didn't ask to be either one. Served time in the slammer on account of both. But that's who I am and I can't deny it."

"How long is this going to take?" Matt asked.

"As long as I need, lieutenant. You can't rush perfection. That's what a Ferguson safe is, perfection."

Matt gave Jake a wary look.

They both stayed in the bedroom while Skinny worked on the safe. After an hour, Matt began to walk through the apartment and Jake started complaining that Skinny didn't know what he was doing. Skinny ignored the complaints and concentrated on his gift. Twenty minutes later, Skinny cracked the safe. He got up from the floor grinning from ear to ear, stuck his hand out, and demanded a hundred dollars.

"You out your damned mind, Skinny. Where you expect me to get a hundred dollars?"

"Give it to him, Jake. He earned it."

Matt emptied the contents of the safe on the bed. He found a will, some stocks and bonds, and a navy blue zippered pouch. When he opened the pouch he found a bill of sale for $22,000 from Herman Wittstein for the purchase of two necklaces. He didn't find the genuine emerald necklace.

"Paydirt, Jake. I found the invoice."

"Great. Let's get out of here."

Matt and Jake took Skinny with them when they paid a visit to Herman Wittstein's shop in Georgetown. Wittstein was closing the shop when they walked in. He was not pleased to see them. Skinny Lester walked around the shop, casing all the jewelry in the display cases. He was impressed by what he saw. Matt confronted Wittstein with the invoice.

"Why didn't you tell me you sold Henry Hughes two fake emerald necklaces, Mr. Wittstein?"

"What was there to tell? He bought the necklaces nearly a year ago. It was a legitimate sale."

"You made those necklaces for Henry Hughes, Wittstein, from the original of the tumbled emerald necklace in the Smithsonian's gem collection, and here's the bill of sale to prove it."

"I didn't make the necklaces, lieutenant. They were ordered from New York City. It's not unusual for customers to order copies of famous jewelry, lieutenant. I get orders like that all the time," Wittstein weakly protested.

"Yes, but you don't get orders for fakes from the chief curator of gems at the Smithsonian which are billed to him personally. That's why you knew Henry Hughes was up to something. So, you put two and two together and decided to blackmail him. That's why he sold you those pieces from the collection for a third of what they were worth. That was the price for your silence."

"That's a dirty lie! I never blackmailed Henry Hughes!"

"The hell you didn't."

"You can't prove anything against me, lieutenant. I have the best lawyers money can buy. The best. Accuse me of blackmailing anybody again and I'll see your ass in court. I mean that."

"The only ass you'll see in court is yours, Wittstein. Henry Hughes stole the genuine emerald necklace and, since you helped him steal it, that makes you an accomplice before and after the fact."

"I placed an order for a customer; and I bought some jewelry he wanted to sell. I did nothing illegal! Nothing! I don't have anything else to say to you, Lieutenant Alexander. Get out of my shop, all of you. Here! Put those chains back," Wittstein shouted at Skinny who was slipping several gold chains into his pocket.

Herman Wittstein ran over to Skinny and pulled a handful of gold chains out of his jeans pocket.

"Man, I was going to pay for these. See here, I got a hundred dollars."

"Hey, man, don't be touching my privates. I don't play that shit," Skinny threatened Wittstein, who was aggressively searching all the pockets in his jeans.

"You got all of them, man. I don't know why you acting like I stole the damned chains when I was getting ready to pay you good money."

"Shut up, Skinny, and get your butt out of here!" Jake shouted as he shoved Skinny through the front door of the shop.

"Man, I ought to kick your scrawny junkie behind. You crazy or something, stealing those chains in front of our faces! We the damned police, you asshole," Jake shouted into Skinny's face as he held him tight by the collar on the sidewalk outside the shop.

"If you so honest, why you ask me to crack that safe?"

"Now, I'm really gonna kick your butt," Jake shouted as he twisted Skinny around and raised his foot.

Skinny shielded his narrow behind with both hands and begged Matt for mercy. Matt doubled over laughing at the sight of Jake holding Skinny by the collar while trying to kick him in the butt with Skinny jumping around like he was doing the St. Vitus dance.

"Let him go, Jake."

"I'm gonna kick this junkie's butt, partner."

"Let him go, man. There's no harm done. Get in the car, Skinny."

Skinny, grinning from ear to ear, jumped into the rear seat of the car. Matt and Jake left Georgetown at six o'clock. They dropped Skinny off at the corner of seat of the car. Matt and Jake left Georgetown at six o'clock. They dropped Skinny off at the corner of Florida and Georgia before returning to headquarters. When he returned to his office, Matt told Jake to follow up on the call to the Thomas family in Greensboro, North Carolina, to see if they really had been visiting Kofi Asante the day after the murder. When Jake made the call, he learned that the Thomases hadn't seen Kofi Asante in over a year.

"I knew he was lying through his teeth, Jake," Matt concluded. "It was a desperate lie, too. He knows something about the murders, man. Why would he be in the museum the morning after the murders, if he wasn't involved in this up to his neck?"

When Matt got back to headquarters, he stopped by Lloyd's office to bring him up to date on the Smithsonian homicides.

"You sure Hughes stole the necklace?"

"No question about it. He wouldn't have caved in to Wittstein's blackmail if he hadn't."

"Stealing emerald necklaces is a far cry from first-degree murder. We still don't know who iced those stiffs, Alexander. Got any ID's on them yet?"

"No. We went ahead and approved the burials."

"Where'd the hell they come from, outer space? We run a first class homicide division and you can't ID two stiffs."

"Sam shot his wad trying to ID the victims, Lloyd. You know how thorough Sam is. If he couldn't find out who they were, nobody can."

"Bullshit! They probably grew up in the District right under our noses."

"We ran their pictures for a month. Nobody from the District identified them. They weren't from here."

"Did you find the murder weapon?"

"Not yet. We checked the District's gun registry against the museum list of employees. Nobody down there registered a twenty-two revolver."

"That's two strikes. What about Henry Hughes? Find him yet?"

"No. He's still missing."

"Three strikes."

"Kendricks and Fisher tried to convince me that Hughes is upset because they fired him, and when he calms down he'll show up. I'm not buying that. He left without cleaning out his office; and his razor and toothbrush and hypertension medicine are still in his bathroom."

"His wife's been talking to the press, lieutenant. They called me today."

"She's worried about her support payment. I need to get someone over to Hughes' condominium to crack a floor safe, Lloyd. We got a warrant to search his place, but we couldn't get into the safe."

"Do you know how much it costs to hire a professional safe-cracker? Why do you have to get into the safe?"

"The people at the Smithsonian are convinced Hughes stole the emerald necklace, too. It may be in his safe. We need to get in there before his wife beats us to the punch."

"Hiring a professional safe-cracker is going to shoot

my budget all to hell. Do you know someone who can do it cheap? He has to be clean, Alexander, no drug addicts or petty thieves."

"Thieves are the only people on the street who know how to crack safes, Lloyd. I know somebody who can do the job real cheap; but he's a thief and an addict."

"Out of the question. I won't authorize hiring anybody like that."

"Give me a hundred dollars out of petty cash and forget about the paper trail."

"I don't want to know who it is or anything else about this operation. You got that?"

"Loud and clear," Matt assured Lloyd as he left Fourth District Headquarters for home.

CHAPTER 14

The following Monday found Willis Brandt presiding at his daily eight-thirty a.m. staff meeting with the museum's security staff.

"Have you found out where that odor is coming from, Simms?"

"No sir. People been complaining about it for a week, but we don't know what's causing it."

"I want to find out what's causing that odor today, Simms. I'm putting you in charge, and I want an answer by the end of the day."

"The odor is circulating through the air vents, chief. We have to search the entire museum to locate it. Who's going to cover for us while we're away from our posts?"

"You figure that out, but I want an answer by the end of the day."

Promptly at noon, Earl Simms and the rest of the security guards detailed to assist him began a systematic search of the second floor. Earl assigned three of the guards to the west side of the floor while he and the two remaining guards took the east side. They searched for over an hour before they reached the Stone Age Mammals exhibit where the odor was very strong, particularly near a diorama depicting stone-age hunters. While he was inspecting the diorama, Earl noticed that the soil covering a shallow mound looked like it had been disturbed. When he took a closer look, he was overwhelmed by the foul odor emanating from the mound. Earl used his portable telephone to call the security guards searching the west side of the floor. They quickly assembled in front of the Ice Age exhibit where Earl pointed to the mound. They spent a few minutes talking the situation over before Earl called Willis Brandt. Brandt arrived promptly. Earl showed him the suspected mound of dirt.

"Dammit Simms, what could be smelling like that?"

"Maybe it's a dead rat, but we've got to move that dirt to find out for sure."

"All right, Simms. Check with maintenance to get the equipment you'll need. Cordon off this area so you don't have visitors moving through here. Jesus, it stinks in here. The sooner you get whatever it is out of there, the better."

Earl and the security guards attacked the mound as soon as shovels and plastic garbage bags arrived from maintenance. Brandt watched from a safe distance as Earl plunged the first shovel into the mound.

Earl gasped when his shovel hit a large solid object just below the surface of the dirt.

"Wait a minute. There's something in here," Earl said as he used his shovel to scrape dirt away from the object he'd struck. The force of his scraping at the bottom of the mound loosened the dirt on top, which cascaded down the mound, revealing a ghastly, decomposed human head. All the guards screamed at the same time.

"God almighty!" Earl screamed. "It's Henry Hughes!"

Willis Brandt ran over to the mound and almost keeled over at the sight of Henry Hughes' blackened, partially decomposed head. Brandt quickly backed away from the mound to a safe corner of the exhibit where he summoned all his strength to keep from vomiting in front of the security guards.

The rest of the guards distanced themselves as far as possible from the decomposing body with its awful stench. Three guards started retching and ran out of the exhibit toward the men's room around the corner.

"Hey, wait a minute. Nobody leaves here until I tell them to," Brandt shouted at the retreating guards.

"Cover him back up, Simms, quick. We've got a serious public health hazard here," Brandt shouted. "Let's keep everything covered until Colonel Kendricks gets here."

Kendricks was totally out of breath by the time he arrived. Brandt had never seen his boss look so desperate. Kendricks headed straight for the mound in the diorama without saying a word to anyone. Everyone's eyes were on him as he told Earl Simms to uncover the body. Earl grimaced as he gingerly shifted the dirt from around the face of the corpse. Kendricks exploded when he saw the face.

"Goddammit it to hell, Brandt! Three murders in your museum! Three!'"

The rest of the security guards were deathly silent. Devastated by Kendricks' attack, Brandt remained silent, too.

"Three murders, Brandt, three. How am I supposed to explain this to the secretary?"

"I don't know, sir. The police have been looking for Henry Hughes for the past 10 days. I don't know when this happened."

"That's just the point. You don't know when the other murders happened, either. This is your museum, Brandt. You're the chief of security. Three murders in three months, and you don't have a clue about what's going on over here. It makes the entire security division look like stupid, incompetent jackasses."

Willis Brandt hung his head and took his whipping, because he knew Kendricks was next in line after the director and the secretary learned that Henry Hughes was lying dead in the museum. Kendricks used Brandt's portable telephone to inform Fisher about the murder. He asked Fisher to call Secretary Marshall, but Fisher adamantly refused. Kendricks placed the call himself. After he hung up, Kendricks told Brandt to call Lieutenant Alexander and the medical examiner's office, so they could remove the body as quickly as possible.

Bill Fisher arrived first. He held a handkerchief to his nose as he walked up to the mound. When he saw Henry Hughes' blackened, decomposed face, he turned red as a beet and ran out of the exhibit through the Mall entrance, where he stood on the steps of the museum gasping for breath as he tried to compose himself. Kendricks ordered the guards to secure all entrances into the east wing of the second floor until the police arrived. Andrew Marshall walked over to the museum alone. He stopped to speak to Fisher, who was still standing on the steps of the museum looking very green about the gills. Fisher advised Marshall not to look at the body, but the secretary insisted on seeing it. Fisher accompanied the secretary as far as the African Bush Elephant in the second-floor rotunda but refused to go back into the exhibit. The secretary was sickened and deeply saddened by what he saw. He asked for a drink of cold water, which Kendricks sent one of the guards to fetch. Then he asked to meet with Fisher, Kendricks, and Brandt in Fisher's office. Kendricks said that Brandt needed to stay near the exhibit until the District Police arrive.

The atmosphere was grim as the three men took the elevator to Fisher's third-floor office at two forty-five Monday afternoon. Fisher told his secretary to make a fresh pot of coffee before he closed the door to his office. Secretary Marshall walked over to the window and looked down on Constitution Avenue. He watched the traffic and pedestrians for a moment before speaking.

"I won't survive Henry's murder, Bill."

"It's not your fault, Andy."

"It's hubris. Henry Hughes hated me while he lived. His death is going to destroy my career. I survived all of his sniping and back stabbing over the years, but I won't survive his death."

Wallace Kendricks wanted to say something reassuring to Andrew Marshall, but he recognized a terrible situation when he saw one. Coming on the heels of the other homicides, Henry Hughes' murder was a devastating blow to Andrew Marshall's leadership of the Smithsonian Institution. Kendricks also knew that the fallout from Hughes' murder would be just as damaging for himself and Fisher, especially for himself. Kendricks figured it would take a major miracle for the secretary to land on his feet after three murders and the theft of the tumbled emerald necklace. Even if Andrew Marshall managed to survive, Kendricks was all but certain that he himself would lose his job as security director. It was clear that Andrew Marshall didn't believe in miracles; and neither did Wallace Kendricks.

"When did you find the body, Wally?"

Kendricks spent the next few minutes briefing the secretary.

An hour later, Matt, Jake, and several other detectives arrived at the crime scene at the same time as Steve Mitchell and the crew from the medical examiner's office. Brandt led them to the body. Steve Mitchell immediately covered the body with a large sheet of thick plastic, evacuated the area, and told his assistant to get their coveralls and oxygen masks from the ambulance.

"Some days it doesn't pay to get up in the morning," Steve Mitchell said to Matt as he waited for his assistant to return with the masks and coveralls.

"Ain't this a bitch," Matt replied. "We've been looking high and low for Henry Hughes for over a week, and he's been laying in here under a pile of dirt the whole time."

"How did he die?" Matt asked Willis Brandt.

"I don't know. After we saw how badly decomposed he was, we covered him back up."

"We've got to get that body out of here quick," Steve told Brandt. "You need to get a decontamination team ready to go in there to clean that place up as soon we move the body. Do you have any procedures in place to handle a situation like this?"

"I've already contacted the District Public Health Department. As soon as they arrive, we'll meet with the head of maintenance so we can get this situation under control."

"Sounds good to me," Steve replied as he took a pair of coveralls and an oxygen mask from his assistant.

"Where are Fisher and Kendricks?" Matt asked Willis Brandt.

"They're upstairs in the director's office with Secretary Marshall."

Matt left Jake in charge of the crime scene and went up to Fisher's office. When he walked into the office, he found the atmosphere as somber as a funeral.

"What happened here, Kendricks?"

"Isn't it obvious that Henry Hughes has been murdered, lieutenant?"

"How was he killed?"

"I don't know. All I know is that Brandt said the staff had been complaining about a strange odor in the museum over the past week. They were looking for what was causing the odor when they found the body this morning."

"If they started smelling him last week, he must have been dead for a while before that. What day did they start smelling the odor?"

"I don't know. You'll have to ask Chief Brandt about that."

"Brandt says the last time Hughes was seen at the

museum was the day he was fired. That was two weeks ago today. My partner and I saw him coming into the museum around seven-thirty when we were leaving that Monday evening. What I want to know is who else did he see at the museum that night?"

"I don't know; but I'll ask Brandt to follow up on that."

"Three murders and you still don't know anything, Kendricks."

"Listen, Alexander, I've had just about enough of your insinuations. I bent over backwards to help you solve those other homicides. If you have a beef with me, let's get it out in the open right here and now," Kendricks angrily shouted.

"Calm down, Wally," the secretary advised Kendricks before turning to Matt. "There's no need to be insulting, lieutenant. All my senior staff have been under enormous pressure since those murders in Natural History this summer, especially Wally Kendricks."

"Well you've got another homicide to deal with now. I told all of you that someone inside the Smithsonian murdered those two men back in June, but you were too busy trying to cover your backsides to listen."

"So why rub our faces in it, now, lieutenant? What's the point?" Fisher asked.

"The point is that if you hadn't been so concerned about controlling the damage to the Smithsonian's reputation, we might have gotten to the bottom of this case before Henry Hughes had to die."

"Are you saying we're responsible for Henry's death?"

the secretary asked.

"What you're responsible for is putting the reputation of the Smithsonian before the lives of the men who were killed. And yes, I do hold you responsible for his death," Matt said before leaving Fisher's office. He returned to the second-floor crime scene, where he found Sam Johnson and Steve Mitchell screaming at each other. Sam accused the deputy medical examiner of altering the crime scene before Sam's forensics team arrived. Steve Mitchell insisted that Hughes' badly decomposed body was a major public health hazard that needed to be moved out of the museum as quickly as possible, despite Sam's strong protests to the contrary. Matt interceded on Sam's behalf. Mitchell and his assistants quit working on the body long enough to allow Sam to take photographs. Matt donned a mask and gloves and walked over to where Steve Mitchell was standing.

"How was he killed, Steve?"

"Multiple stab wounds throughout the chest cavity and the abdomen. There's a large contusion on the back of the head, too. He was probably hit with a heavy object and knocked unconscious before he was stabbed."

"No bullet wounds?"

"None that I saw."

"What was he stabbed with?"

"A sharp pointed object, some type of knife. His wrists and ankles are bound."

"You mean he was tied up?"

"Yes. He must have been knocked unconscious, tied

up, and carried to that mound. From the amount of bleeding on his clothes and on the floor around the body, it's a good bet he was killed after his body was placed in the mound."

"How long has he been dead?" Matt asked.

"At least 10 days or more, from the extent of the decomposition. I'll be able to tell you more after I get the body back to the morgue."

While Matt and Steve were talking, Secretary Marshall walked into the exhibit and asked Matt to meet him in his office as soon as possible. Matt agreed. Sam finished taking pictures of the crime scene. Steve Mitchell and his assistants wrapped the body in plastic, placed it in a body bag, and left. Matt conferred with Jake and Sam for several minutes before leaving for Andrew Marshall's office in the Castle.

"Thanks for coming, lieutenant. Please, sit down."

"What did you want to talk to me about?"

"How was Henry killed?"

"Multiple stab wounds to the chest and abdomen."

The color left the secretary's face as he got up from his desk and walked over to the large window on the west side of his office.

"I'm still trying to make sense out of these murders, lieutenant. If anyone had told me that three people could be murdered in the Museum of Natural History, I would have told them they weren't playing with a full deck. People like to work in museums, Lieutenant Alexander. The pay is bad, usually, but the work is stimulating and the atmosphere is genteel . . . civilized. That's what so bizarre about these murders. They're so uncivilized, so barbaric. I can't understand it."

"Murders happen every day, Mr. Secretary. They're as common as dirt in the District. People kill each other all the time for very trivial reasons. Human life is cheap in the District of Columbia. I wish to God it wasn't, but it is."

"I used to think the Smithsonian was different from the rest of the District, lieutenant. I thought we offered a haven from all the madness infesting the crime-ridden areas of this city. I liked to believe that anyone could come to one of our museums and get some respite from whatever was troubling them. That the civility and sanity of the museum environments would be a relief from the violence and chaos they encounter on the streets. It looks like I was wrong, because someone brought that chaos and madness in here."

"You're assuming that the murders were committed by someone from outside the museum, Mr. Secretary. I think you're wrong."

"I don't believe one of our staff people killed three people, lieutenant."

"Henry Hughes was involved in the murders up to his eyeballs, if he didn't kill those two men himself. I have solid proof he paid Herman Wittstein to order those fake emerald necklaces. Wittstein guessed Hughes planned to steal the tumbled emerald necklace because Hughes paid for the reproductions himself. So Wittstein blackmailed Hughes into selling him the antique jewelry from your collection at one-third of what it was worth."

"Doesn't that give Mr. Wittstein a motive for killing Henry?" The secretary asked as he left the window and sat down in the chair across from Matt.

"I'm not ruling him out."

"Henry Hughes was a sick man, lieutenant, brilliant but sick. His personality got increasingly brittle as he got older. When he came to the Smithsonian 12 years ago, he was so optimistic about his future here. I was assistant secretary for museums at the time, and I personally supported hiring Henry despite the poor recommendations he received from the Chemistry Department at the university where he worked. Henry was my roommate at Harvard. I believed he could turn his career around at the Smithsonian, too.

"Things went along pretty well for about five years. Henry adjusted well at Natural History at first and he was eventually promoted to chief curator of the gem collection. I don't know when things started to sour, but I suspect he began to resent the fact that my career was going so well and his wasn't. That's when he broke off his relationship with me and started leaking negative information on the Hill. Henry's from *the* Hughes family, lieutenant. His family's very old, and very rich. He knows, knew I should say, a lot of influential congressmen; and after I became secretary, he regularly used his connections to undermine my leadership here." The secretary's comments trailed off.

"Wittstein said he placed the necklace order nearly a year ago, so Hughes had been planning the theft for some time. I'm convinced Henry Hughes is the key to the other murders, and he must have had an accomplice inside the museum who murdered him for the necklace."

"Henry must have been out of his mind. There have been rumors about Henry's emotional stability among the senior staff, especially after his divorce. He bought a condominium somewhere in Georgetown and refused to give personnel his new address and telephone number. His wife, Jean, finally gave it to them after she got tired of getting his mail. He was furious when he found out we had his new address. There's no doubt that Henry was getting more and more eccentric. And then there was the situation with those maintenance men in Natural History."

"You mean Kofi Asante and Carlos Williams?"

"Yes. Henry insisted that we fire Kofi Asante, but he didn't have a leg to stand on, since he started the fight. Several people witnessed the incident. So the only thing we could do was reprimand Asante."

Andrew Marshall's secretary stepped inside the office door to tell him that his four o'clock appointment was waiting. Matt got up to leave, though he sensed that the secretary would like to talk longer. When he got back to the museum, he found Sam, Lois, and Ruby processing the crime scene while Jake and the other District Police officers were milling around shooting the breeze. Matt ordered them all to start looking for the knife that was used to kill Henry Hughes. Then Matt walked over to speak to Chief Brandt, who looked drained and dazed.

"When my partner and I left the museum after

searching Hughes' office on Monday two weeks ago, Brandt, we saw him enter the museum around seven-thirty that evening. Do you know what he was doing here?"

"I remember seeing him come in that night. I guessed he was cleaning out his office, lieutenant, because the director had fired him that morning."

"The deputy medical examiner says Hughes has been dead at least 10 to 14 days, Brandt. You need to get busy finding out who was in the museum during second and third-shifts that Monday night, because it's shaping up like Hughes was killed the same day he was fired."

Brandt looked grim as Matt left him and walked over to where Sam was examining the dirt and the floor where the body had lain.

"What have you found so far, Sam?"

"Not much, Alexander. There's a lot of blood in the dirt and on the floor," Sam said as he pointed out dark, dried blood stains. "Look at these small dents in the floor here."

Matt leaned over Sam's shoulder to see what Sam was pointing to.

"What are they?"

"Looks like they were made by the tip of a knife being plunged into the floor."

"Damn! Somebody wanted to make sure Hughes was dead, Sam."

"You got that right."

"Find anything else?"

"Lois and Ruby are processing the diorama, but I

doubt if they'll find anything over there," Sam said, looking toward the rear of the diorama where the two criminalists were working. See how this mound is isolated from the rest of the diorama?"

Matt stood up and looked around.

"Yeah, I see what you mean."

"The killer probably moved the dirt from on top of the mound, laid Hughes' unconscious body at the bottom of the mound, stabbed him to death, and covered him up. There was no need for him to leave prints all over the diorama. The killer took the weapon with him when he left; and he made sure it didn't drip or splatter any blood outside the mound. He's smart, Alexander. This crime scene isn't going to tell us much."

"Keep looking, Sam. I need something linking the killer to the crime scene."

"It doesn't look promising," Sam concluded as he continued to sift through the dirt.

Matt walked over to where Lois and Ruby were dusting for prints around a hunting scene where three hunters, two standing and one crouching, were depicted pursuing a stuffed bison. One of the hunters held a long spear with a foot-long blade in his upraised arm as he prepared to launch it at the bison. Matt examined the spear closely. It was firmly attached to the hunter's hand. The other standing hunter was depicted with a taut bow and drawn arrow while the hunter crouching in the grass looked out for prey. Matt noted the relation of the rest of the diorama to the bloody mound where Hughes' decayed body had been discovered.

Later, Matt and Jake left the crime scene for Willis Brandt's office, where Brandt gave them the employee rosters and sign-in logs for second and third-shifts the Monday Hughes was fired. One of the first names Matt read from the list was Kofi Asante. He noted Carlos Johnson's name farther down the list. "Were all of these employees on duty September eleventh?"

"I have no idea. You'll have to check with personnel to see who was here and who wasn't."

Matt and Jake left the Museum of Natural History at six o'clock.

"Where to?" Jake asked.

"Back to headquarters. I want to begin the report on Hughes' homicide tonight, so I can brief Lloyd first thing in the morning. I'm closing this case this week, Jake."

"How can you do that when you don't know who the murderer is, man?"

"Watch me."

Once he got to his office, Matt began the homicide report on Henry Hughes. When he finished, he read through all the information on the Smithsonian homicides again. Although several critical questions remained unanswered, he knew without a doubt how the tumbled emerald necklace was stolen. He left headquarters at midnight.

CHAPTER 15

The following Tuesday morning, Matt headed for D.C. General Hospital to pick up the preliminary post-mortem report on Henry Hughes from the deputy medical examiner. He read the report in Steve's office, noting that the cause and time of death had changed very little from Steve's original assessment at the crime scene. The report stated that Henry Hughes had been dead approximately 14 days which put the time of death very close to the last Monday evening he was seen at the museum. The same day he was fired by Fisher. The post-mortem report also indicated that the murder had been committed with a large, sharp-bladed instrument.

"I've got a present for you, Matt," Steve said.

"As long as it's not pickled in formaldehyde."

Steve unlocked his desk drawer and handed Matt a .22-caliber revolver in a plastic bag.

"Where'd you get this gun?"

"Off Hughes' corpse. It was in the right hand pocket of his sports jacket."

"You just pulled my fat from the fire, Steve."

"You think it's the weapon used on those stiffs in June?"

"Hell, yes, I think it's the weapon. All Sam has to do

is match it against the markings on the slugs you took from their bodies. Man, you just made my day."

"You owe me one, lieutenant."

"Don't I know it."

"Tell Sam to handle that weapon in the ventilator hood because it came directly from the body. I didn't want to fumigate it because of the prints."

"Tell me about the weapon that was used on Hughes, Steve."

"It was a large, tapered blade about eight to 10 inches long and three inches at its widest point. The blade was heavy and smooth on the edges. The killer plunged the blade into Hughes with a lot of force. Hughes was still alive when the killer began stabbing him. The blow to the back of his head knocked him unconscious, so he was easy to kill. There were several broken ribs and crushed vertebrae. My guess is that the assailant probably used both hands to plunge the blade into Hughes' body. There are exactly 15 stab wounds, three of them through the heart. The rest were scattered throughout the chest cavity and the abdomen. There were also a series of seven to eight glancing thrusts that didn't go very deep because the angle of the blade was too steep for penetration, but they did leave significant abrasions and contusions."

"How long did it take him to die?"

"He died instantly after he got the first stab through the heart. There were three stabs to the heart and each one of them was sufficient to kill immediately."

Matt took the preliminary post mortem report when he left Steve Mitchell's office at nine o'clock. He drove back to headquarters where he left the revolver taken off Henry Hughes' body with Sam Johnson. Afterward, he met with Lloyd Cullison to brief him on the Hughes homicide. Lloyd was upset to learn there had been another murder at the Smithsonian when they hadn't solved the first two homicides, but he was pleased to learn that the Hughes revolver was the likely murder weapon.

"How're you gonna pin the murders on a corpse, Alexander?"

"We establish it's Henry Hughes' revolver, it's in the bag. Since Hughes or his accomplice planted one of the fake necklaces he had Herman Wittstein order for him on the body, it stands to reason that he was the one who killed them."

"Maybe the accomplice killed Hughes and the two stiffs who tried to steal the necklace and then planted the gun on Hughes."

"If that person used a revolver the first time, why not the second time? Henry Hughes died of multiple stab wounds, Lloyd. We're dealing with two different MO's and two different murderers; and I'll stake my reputation Henry Hughes did the first two. Remember, he ordered the necklaces from Wittstein and sold him the antique jewelry, too."

"I'm waiting to see what Sam's ballistics results say, Alexander. You got any proof it's Hughes gun?"

"Not yet. The gun isn't registered, but his wife may be able to identify it."

"Looks like you've still got some homework to do, lieutenant."

"Sam's checking the revolver for prints, too. We got Henry Hughes' prints from the bonding company that insures staff at the Smithsonian. If his prints show up on the weapon, and if the ballistics tests are consistent with the markings on the slugs from the June homicide victims, I'll be satisfied."

"What about the weapon that killed Hughes?"

"We haven't found it; and we searched hard for it. But that's a mother of a museum. Sam even checked the spear in the diorama, but there was no trace of blood on it. Looks like the killer took the weapon with him."

"Keep me posted, Alexander. Looks like you might close this case after all."

After he left Lloyd's office, Matt wondered about the weapon used to kill Henry Hughes. Matt had sent Jake back to the Museum of Natural History early Tuesday morning to continue searching for the weapon, but it didn't look promising. If the killer was smart enough not to leave any traces of his presence at the scene, it wasn't likely that he would have discarded the murder weapon inside the museum. Matt dropped into Sam's office in the crime lab before he left for the Smithsonian.

"You're just like a bad penny, Alexander. You keep turning up."

"Why do you think the killer didn't leave any evidence at the scene, Sam?"

"I've been thinking about that myself. There should have been splatter and trace evidence around the mound, but there wasn't. It was as clean as a whistle."

"How do you explain that Sam?"

"Easy. The floor around the mound had been systematically cleaned. When you go back down there, compare how clean the floor area around the mound is to the rest of the floor in the diorama which is as dusty as hell. Whoever killed Hughes made sure they erased all their tracks at the crime scene."

Matt pondered Sam's words as he drove downtown. When he arrived at the Museum of Natural History, he returned to the scene of Henry Hughes' murder and walked through the diorama again. He noted the stone age weapons still held by two hunters and felt a nagging worry that he had missed something. He studied the crime scene for some time before he went downstairs to Willis Brandt's office and asked him for the name of the curator who had developed the Stone Age Mammals exhibit. Brandt took him to Martha Darden's office. Martha remembered Matt from their earlier encounter.

"I simply can't get my mind around the fact that Henry Hughes is dead, Lieutenant Alexander. I don't understand any of this. What's happening to our museum?"

"Murders go on outside your museum everyday, Miss Darden. More people die violently in a week in Anacostia than in Chevy Chase or Bethesda in 20 years. Welcome to the club."

"What did you want to know about the Stone Age Mammals exhibit?"

"It's hard to say, since I don't know the answer to that question myself, Miss Darden. What can you tell me about the exhibit?"

"It's over 10 years old. The curator who supervised its development no longer works at the museum. I guess I'm the most senior person left at the museum who worked on it."

"Did you design it?"

"No, I didn't. But I was responsible for researching parts of the exhibit and for identifying artifacts from the Native American collection."

"What type of artifacts, Miss Darden?"

"All types consistent with how hunter-gatherers lived during that time period. If I remember correctly, we used pottery, basketry, animal skin clothing, weapons, and other items."

"What type of weapons?"

"Whatever you see in the exhibit. I can't remember everything I identified. What does this have to do with Henry's death?"

"I don't know yet. Will you come downstairs and walk through the exhibit with me? Maybe that will refresh your memory."

Martha Darden led Matt down to the exhibit through the back way. Matt showed her where the body had been found and explained the type of knife Steve Mitchell said had been used to kill Henry Hughes. Martha was visibly disturbed by the violent imagery of the knife being plunged into Henry Hughes' chest over and over again. She shivered and quickly walked past the site where the mound had been. Matt followed while Martha took her time walking through the diorama.

"It's amazing how much time and effort you spend developing an exhibit and how quickly you forget how much work was actually involved. I spent two years on this exhibit, and I never worked harder in my life."

"Do you notice anything different, Miss Darden?"

"Well, the mound is missing, but other than that everything looks the same to me," Martha said as she walked past the three hunters stalking the buffalo. Wait a minute. Something is missing."

"What?"

Martha pointed to the crouching hunter.

"His spear is missing. It was lying on the grass beside him, but I don't see it now."

"Can you describe the spear?"

"It was an exact copy of that one," Martha replied as she pointed to the spear being held aloft by the standing hunter. I remember I had two spears fabricated. We were supposed to get three standing hunters from the exhibit fabricators, but one hunter came back crouching and I had no choice but to lay his spear on the ground beside him. It's not there anymore."

"When was the last time you were in the diorama?"

"It's been so long ago, I don't remember."

"Does anyone else keep track of the artifacts in here?"

"Not really. Just look at the accumulation of dust all over everything."

Matt walked over to the standing hunter holding the other spear.

"Is there any way you can remove this spear from his hand?"

"No, you can't. The spear was so heavy we had to permanently attach it to the hand and floor because it kept toppling the hunter over. I doubt if we can remove it without damaging the mannequin."

Matt thanked Martha Darden for her help. As he drove back to headquarters, he thought about the missing spear. He was convinced that the spear had been used to kill Henry Hughes, but he didn't understand why the killer had taken the spear with him. If what Sam said was true, the killer had spent a lot of time cleaning the crime scene. Why not clean the spear and put it back where he got it?

CHAPTER 16

"Excuse me, sir, I'm looking for my son and my nephew. The last letter I got from them had this address on the envelope."

Willie Taylor, the proprietor of the Washington Arms Single-Room Occupancy Hotel, looked up from his morning paper to find a tiny, middle-aged, soft-spoken black woman facing him from across the counter. She looked dead tired, but both the Washington Arms Hotel and its proprietor had seen better days, too. Viola Jones tried not to stare at the dirty floor with its cracked and missing tiles, at the torn carpet runners, at the soiled windows, at the broken down furniture in the lobby, or at Willie Taylor for that matter, who was in desperate need of a shave and a clean shirt.

"What's your son's name?"

"Walter Jones. His cousin's name is Eddie Jones," she replied. "I haven't heard from them in a long time. We don't have any relatives in Washington, D.C. That's why I came up here to see if they're all right."

"You say they staying here?"

"Yes sir. The last letter I got from them had this address on it."

"That thieving clerk I hired up and left for California last week. He took a whole month's receipts with him," Willie lied as he gave Viola Jones a sly glance to see if she was buying it. "Wait a minute while I check my records," he continued as he leafed through an ancient, dog-eared ledger.

"Here they are. Walter and Eddie Jones, Room 415. They been gone over three months. Beat me out of a month's rent before they left, too. When you find them two, you tell' em I done turned their bill over to a collection agency. They going to jail if I don't get my money. You tell' em Willie Taylor wants his money when you find them, lady."

"My name is Viola Jones, Mr. Taylor. How much money did they owe you?" she asked as she opened her purse to make good her son's debt.

"A hundred and fifty between them. I let the both of them rent that room for the price of one. I get $300 a month for single rooms at the Washington Arms. I let the both of them have that room for the price of one; and they still walked away without paying me."

Viola Jones looked defeated when she heard how much her son and nephew owed Willie Taylor. She reluctantly took a crumpled twenty dollar bill out of her coin purse and handed it to Willie Taylor who, while less than impressed, took the money anyway.

"I can't pay the whole amount right now, Mr. Taylor, but here's twenty dollars on account. I'll send you the rest when I get back to South Carolina."

"I'm against partial payments, Mrs. Jones, but I'll take it just this once because you look like an honest woman, which is more than I can say for your son and nephew."

"They're good boys, Mr. Taylor. If they didn't pay you, it's because they didn't have the money. Did they tell you where they were going when they left?"

"If they had told me, I've have put the law on them a long time ago. They just walked away one day back in June and never showed up again. Left all their things behind, too. I kept the room for a week, then I packed their clothes in a box and put the box in the basement."

"Can I have their clothes?"

"No ma'am, you can't. That box of clothes is my insurance. They get the clothes when I get the rest of my money."

"You said they've been gone since June?"

"Yeah, that's right. They left near the second week in June. I lost a whole month's rent on that room because of them."

"Gone three months! Lord! Where can those children be?"

"You say you don't have any relatives in the District?"

"No, I don't."

"Where you staying?"

"I haven't had time to look for a place to stay yet. I got off the greyhound bus at eight o'clock this morning and came right over here. I worked all day yesterday in the chicken processing plant and rode that Greyhound bus all night. I just have to find those children, Mr. Taylor."

"I got a vacant room, Mrs. Jones. I'll rent it to you if you want it," Willie Taylor generously offered despite himself.

"I can't afford your rates," Mrs. Jones insisted as she gripped her worn black leather purse.

"How much were you looking to pay for a room in D.C.?"

"I can't pay no more than $50 by the week."

"Well, I normally charges $75 by the week, but since you seem like such a nice lady, I'll let you have the room for $50."

"I don't want to take advantage of your kindness, Mr. Taylor, but I need a room awful bad. I'll take it."

Willie Taylor handed Viola Jones her key and showed her how to get up to her room on the second floor of the Washington Arms.

"My son said he had found work in his last letter; but he didn't mention who he was working for. Do you know who he was working for, Mr. Taylor?"

"No ma'am, I don't. He never mentioned his job to me."

"Where's the nearest police station from here, Mr. Taylor?"

"You go out to Georgia Avenue and take an uptown bus to Fourth District Police Headquarters. It's five miles up Georgia Avenue, Mrs. Jones. You can't miss it."

With a heavy heart, Viola Jones carried her small suitcase up the stairs to her second floor room. Later that afternoon, she caught the bus to Fourth District Headquarters, where she filed missing persons reports on her son and her nephew. She then went back to her hotel room and started calling hospitals throughout the city.

At noon the next day she received a call asking her to return to Fourth District Headquarters to provide more information on the missing persons reports she had filed on Walter and Eddie Jones. When Viola Jones arrived at headquarters, she was escorted to Matt and Jake's office on the second floor. Both detectives stood up when she entered the office. Matt introduced himself and his partner. Viola looked frightened but determined to find out where Walter and Eddie were. She took the chair Matt offered her.

"We were given these missing persons reports on Walter Jones and Eddie Jones this morning, Mrs. Jones. How long have they been missing?"

Viola Jones opened her purse, removed a letter, and handed it to Matt.

"This is the last letter I got from Walter. It was written back in May. I haven't heard from him since then, Lieutenant Alexander. Yesterday morning, when I got to the hotel where they had been staying, Mr. Willie Taylor told me they had been gone since the second week of June."

"The letter is dated May twenty-fifth," Matt said, looking at Jake. "Who is Willie Taylor, Mrs. Jones?"

"He runs the hotel where Walter and Eddie were staying. I took a room there, too, until I find my boys."

Jake and Matt looked at each other. Jake avoided looking at Viola Jones.

"Mr. Taylor said they just up and left one day without even taking their things. Now, isn't that peculiar, lieutenant? Where could they have gone that they wouldn't need clothes?"

Jake began to make nervous fidgeting movements.

"How old were they?"

"Walter is the oldest. He's 23. Eddie's four years

younger than Walter, so that makes him 19. He'll be 20 years old on his birthday coming up December sixteenth. I raised them like they were brothers, even though they're just cousins. Eddie's my sister Doris' boy. Doris was killed by Eddie's father when Eddie was just six months old. I took him and raised him just like he was my own after his mother was shot to death. They're good boys, lieutenant. I raised them to be decent, god-fearing boys, and they never gave me cause to be ashamed, neither one of them."

"Where you from, Mrs. Jones?"

"I'm from Georgetown, South Carolina. Walter and Eddie lived with me in Georgetown until they decided to come to D.C. to find jobs back in the spring. They both worked in the chicken processing plant in Georgetown for a couple of years. I work there myself. It pays okay but it's nasty work and not much of a future for young people."

"Exactly when did they come to the District?"

"They left the day after Easter Sunday. Walter came to Washington, D.C. on his senior class trip, and he took a real liking to it. He always talked about coming back here to live. He liked the fact that black folks had good jobs in Washington, D.C."

"You said they were living at the Washington Arms on Georgia and Ninth?"

"Yes, that's right."

"Sergeant Jackson and I are homicide detectives, Mrs. Jones," Matt explained as he got up from his desk and carried a file folder over to Viola Jones. He pulled up another chair beside her. "We've been tracking missing persons reports since the second week in June to try to identify two young black men. I don't want to upset you Mrs. Jones; and these may not be the boys you're looking for. But, I have to tell that these young men were killed in the Museum of Natural History without any identification on them."

Viola Jones' screams filled the office with the dread and pain of a mother who knew she would never see her child again. Loud sobs wracked her small body and resonated through the office, making Jake so nervous he got up and left the room. Matt gave her his handkerchief. She cried against his shoulder for several minutes before she began to calm down.

"Do you think you're able to look at these pictures, Mrs. Jones?"

Viola Jones nodded her agreement with her eyes still closed. Matt opened the folder. When she finally opened her eyes and saw the pictures of Walter and Eddie, Viola howled as if she had been stabbed through the heart with a red-hot poker. She jumped up from her chair, sending the contents of the file folder flying across the floor. In her agitation, she knocked her chair to the floor and flung her purse onto Jake's desk.

"My babies are dead!" she screamed. "My babies are dead!"

Matt jumped up to avoid her flailing arms and upset his chair, too. Her screams brought several officers into the second floor corridor outside Matt's office where Jake was standing a safe distance from the turmoil. They peered through the glass door into the office where they saw Matt trying to comfort Viola Jones, who stood rigidly in the middle of the floor screaming and beseeching God for comfort. Matt looked angrily through the glass door to where Jake was standing in the corridor with a helpless look on his face. Matt righted Viola's chair and got her to sit down again. She stopped screaming, but her face was still drenched in tears and her small body was wracked with sobs. Matt left her long enough to tell Jake to fetch her a cup of black coffee.

"What's happened to my children's' bodies, lieutenant?" Viola asked in a hoarse whisper.

"The District buried them, Mrs. Jones. We ran their pictures in all the local papers and tried to wait until somebody claimed the bodies."

"Where are they buried?"

"I'll find out for you, Mrs. Jones."

"I have to go and see my children, lieutenant. I have to go."

"I'll take you to the cemetery myself."

Jake returned with hot coffee for Viola. She was too upset to drink it. Matt picked the pictures up from the floor. Viola stopped crying and just rocked in the chair with her eyes closed. When she opened them, she asked, "How were Walter and Eddie killed, Lieutenant Alexander?"

"They were shot to death."

"Lord have mercy! Shot down like dogs! Who did it?"

"We don't yet know who shot them. Now that we've found out who they are and where they lived, we'll be able to find out who killed them, Mrs. Jones. I promise you that."

"Shot like dogs! Lord have mercy on my children!" Viola cried softly into Matt's handkerchief.

"What do you know about Walter and Eddie's life after they came to the District, Mrs. Jones?"

"They hadn't been able to find any jobs. They had just about run out of money, too. I sent them $75 in May; but I told them they might as well come on back home and get their old jobs back. But Eddie didn't want to come back. He was determined to stay in Washington, D.C. Walter mentioned that he had found a job in his last letter, but he didn't say where it was."

"Did he mention whether they had made any friends in the District?"

"No, he didn't mention any friends."

After Viola Jones calmed down, Matt and Jake took her back to the Washington Arms hotel. Jake had agreed to take Viola Jones' home with him so he escorted her up to her room to pack while Matt confronted Willie Taylor about the box of clothing belonging to the victims.

"I can't let you have that box until I get the rest of my money, Lieutenant Alexander. I'm out three hundred dollars for that room," Willie lied.

"When was the last time this dump was inspected for fire code violations?" Matt asked.

"So, it's gonna be like that, huh?" Willie Taylor asked.

"You're damned right it's gonna be like that. Where's that box of clothes, Taylor?"

"I can't leave the front desk. There's nobody here to relieve me."

"I'll watch the desk for you."

Five minutes later, Willie Taylor came back carrying the large box of clothes. Matt took the box and headed for his car, which was illegally parked in front of the hotel. He waited for Viola Jones and Jake, who emerged with her suitcase several minutes later. They drove over to Jake's house and left Viola Jones with Jake's wife, Florence.

After they returned to headquarters, Matt carried the box to their office, where he and Jake searched through its contents. Jake was sorting through the papers and magazines at the bottom of the box when he found a flier from the Ife Temple.

"Have mercy, partner! We nailed them this time!" Jake shouted as he handed Matt the flier.

"Hot damn!" Matt shouted. I knew this case would break this week."

"What now?" Jake asked.

"We've got to get a warrant from Judge Parham to search the temple. Let's go."

They arrived at the Ife Temple three hours later at seven-thirty in the evening. The guard who opened the door informed them that Kofi and Carlos had already left for work and refused to let them in. Matt showed him the warrant. The guard still refused to let them in. After calling for reinforcements, Matt waited. Fifteen minutes later, three squad cars filled with 10 uniformed officers arrived. Matt knocked on the door again, this time backed up by the 10 officers. The guard let them in. Kofi's wife, Miriam, met them in the alcove of the temple. Matt showed her the warrant.

"Why do you want to search the temple, Lieutenant Alexander? What have we done?"

"For starters, you lied about knowing Walter and Eddie Jones. Both of them had been to the Ife Temple, but all of you said you had never seen either one of them."

"We can't remember everybody who comes here, lieutenant. Plenty of people come once and never come back. You can't expect us to remember every single person who has ever come to the temple."

"Walter and Eddie Jones came here more than once. That's why they ended up shot to death in the Museum of Natural History where your husband, Kofi Asante, works."

"Kofi didn't have anything to do with those killings. He would never harm anybody."

"Tell it to the judge, Mrs. Asante. I'm here to execute a search warrant."

"What are you searching for?"

"A murder weapon, for starters," Matt replied, dismissing Miriam Asante and turning to Jake and the other officers.

"Where do you want us to start looking?" Jake asked.

"Put half of the officers upstairs and the other half down here."

Matt told Miriam to assemble all the residents of the house in the meeting room of the temple while officers searched for the murder weapon. She quickly rounded the occupants up, despite strong objections, especially from the children.

The search began in earnest about eight o'clock. Matt and five other officers searched the eight rooms on the second floor of the house. They found nothing related to the murders. Afterwards, they went up to the third floor of the temple, where they again came up empty-handed. Jake and the officers in the lower half of the house searched the first floor and the basement with nothing to show for their efforts, either. Matt went back downstairs. He and Jake conferred in the temple foyer.

"We didn't find anything, partner. What about you?"

"Nothing looking like a spear."

"They got a whole lot of African shit around here, but there ain't one spear in the whole joint."

"It's here all right. We just haven't found it yet."

"Yeah, well, how long we supposed to look?"

"We'll wait for Asante and Williams. Did you send a squad car after them?"

"Yeah. They ought to getting back pretty soon."

"You taking them in?"

"Got to. They killed Henry Hughes," Matt replied as the officers detailed to pick up Kofi and Carlos ushered the suspects through the front door of the temple, their hands handcuffed behind their backs.

"What you mean having us arrested off our jobs, man? Those racist crackers at the museum been looking for a reason to fire us. You a black man. Why you fucking us over like this?" Carlos demanded.

"I'm a cop, Williams. You think being black gives you the right to snuff somebody?"

"We didn't kill nobody, man! How many times do I have to tell you that?" Kofi shouted.

"Walter and Eddie Jones were members of the Ife Temple. You put them up to breaking into the museum; Henry Hughes caught them in the museum that night trying to steal the emerald necklace and he killed them. Then you killed Henry Hughes. All I want to know from you is where is the emerald necklace and where is the spear you used to kill Hughes. They're both here in the temple."

Kofi and Carlos faced Matt from across the foyer, the dim ceiling light casting shadows between them. Carlos said nothing, as he stared at Matt through fierce, hate-filled eyes.

"I would never kill another human being, lieutenant. I'm not that kind of person. I did help Walter and Eddie break into the museum to steal the emerald necklace; but I didn't kill Henry Hughes. The last time I saw him, he was alive," Kofi insisted.

"When was the last time you saw Henry Hughes, Asante?"

"The same day he was fired. He was in his office that Monday evening about eight o'clock. Carlos and I were cleaning his office suite when he walked in on us. He got real mad and told us to get the hell out of his office. He just kept on talking to us like we were dirt under his feet. Then he pulled a gun on us. He told us that if we didn't get out of his office, we'd end up shot just like our friends. Man when he said that, I clocked on that racist. I just turned around and decked him right in his office because I knew he had killed Walter and Eddie. He fell back and hit his head on the corner of his credenza; but he was alive. I checked his pulse to be sure."

"So what happened next?"

"When he fell back, the necklace slipped out of his coat pocket onto the floor, so we took the necklace and put the gun back in his pocket. Then we left him in his office. We figured that even if he came to he couldn't accuse us of stealing the necklace from him, since he was the one who stole it from the museum in the first place."

"You know damned well he was going to report you for attacking him, Asante. That's why you killed him."

"Give me a break, lieutenant. He pulled a gun on us; but we didn't kill him. I'm telling you the truth. We didn't kill him. Carlos and I left him laying in his office; and that's the last I ever saw of him."

"Where did you go after you left Hughes in his office?"

"I went downstairs to the first floor to clean the Associates Dining Room and Carlos went down to the second floor to clean the west wing."

"Isn't the Stone Age Mammals exhibit in the West Wing of the second floor?"

"Yeah, I guess so."

"How long did you clean the exhibit, Williams?"

Carlos refused to answer Matt.

"Tell him how long you took to clean the West Wing, Carlos," Kofi insisted.

Carlos still refused to answer.

Kofi frowned as he tried to remember.

"I didn't see him again until we checked out. I remember asking Carlos why he stayed on the second floor so long."

"Why you trying to hang me out to dry?" Carlos shouted at Kofi. "I stuck with you through thick and thin all these years. I was the one who saved your pretty ass when you was in Lorton and the first chance you get you throw me to the wolves. You owe me big time; and this is how you repay me?" Carlos screamed as he vented his wrath on Kofi.

"Why did you stay on the second floor so long, Williams?" Matt asked.

Matt, Jake, Kofi, and the other officers all looked at Carlos.

"None of your damned business, Jack. You know so much, you tell me why."

"Your friend here killed Henry Hughes, Asante. He shifted the dirt from that mound in the Stone Age Mammals exhibit. Then he went back upstairs to Hughes' office, tied Hughes up, put him in his cleaning cart, and rolled his cart back to the second floor, where he placed Hughes' body in the mound. After that, he took a spear he found in the exhibit and stabbed Hughes 15 times, three times through the heart, covered his body up, and left him there. Isn't that right, Williams?"

"I ain't killed nobody. But that son-of-a-bitch Hughes killed Walter and Eddie. What goes around comes around. That's all I got to say."

"You let Walter and Eddie into the museum, didn't

"You let Walter and Eddie into the museum, didn't you, Asante?"

"Yeah, we let them in at the start of the second-shift before the museum closed. They stayed in a closet in the supply room until after the second-shift ended at midnight. Then they changed clothes and went up to the third floor to steal the necklace. After they stole the necklace, they were supposed to go back to the supply closet, change clothes, and stay there until the museum opened Wednesday morning. Then they were supposed to leave the museum and come back to the Ife Temple. When they were late showing up here, I went down to the museum to see what had happened. That's when I found out they had been murdered. I hung around the diorama for a few minutes, and then I went down to the closet in the supply room to get the clothes they had left in there and I came back to the temple."

"What was the point of them dressing like African warriors?"

"One of the members of the temple from Zambia taught them how to cast a spell to steal the emerald necklace. He said the spell wouldn't work if they wore American clothes, so he made them dress like African warriors."

"Let me get this straight, Asante. You actually believe Walter and Eddie Jones stole the emerald necklace from the gem collection, using a voodoo spell?"

"Didn't you find the necklace on Walter's body?"

"Listen, man. After you stole the necklace from Hughes, didn't you wonder about that other emerald necklace in the display case?"

"No, I didn't wonder about it."

"You should have. Walter and Eddie didn't steal the genuine emerald necklace, Asante. Their so-called voodoo spell wasn't worth a damn against the gem collection's security system. Henry Hughes stole that necklace."

"Henry Hughes was an evil man," Kofi replied.

"So where's the necklace, Asante?"

"It's upstairs. I'll show you if you take these cuffs off me."

Matt told one of the uniformed officers to remove Kofi's cuffs. Then Matt, Jake, and three officers followed Kofi upstairs to the third floor where he led them to a loose floor board under the rug. When Kofi removed the necklace, he also pulled out an elaborately decorated vest covered in gold chains, and dozens of precious and semi-precious stones, including one of the large tumbled emeralds from the necklace. He handed Matt the necklace, which had been cut through.

" I can't believe you stole a $10 million necklace to put it on this thing!" Matt said.

"The only reason we wanted the necklace in the first place was to get one of the emeralds for the High Priest's breastplate."

"For what?"

"The High Priest's breastplate," Kofi repeated, holding the vest up for Matt to see before slowly putting it on. We had collected every stone but the emerald."

"What's so special about the High Priest's breastplate that you'd risk going back to jail, Asante?"

"The stones of the breastplate of the High Priest are sacred to the 12 angels that guard the gates of paradise, Lieutenant Alexander. God announces victory in battle through the light emanating from the 12 stones worn by the High Priest on the Breastplate of Judgment."

"So what does any of that have to do with you, Asante. You're not a Jew."

"The High Priest of Memphis in Egypt wore the Breastplate of Judgment in 4000 B.C. The breastplate came from Egypt just like the Eye of Ra over the temple door. There is great power in the Eye of Ra, lieutenant; and there is great power in the breastplate of Judgment."

"You don't really believe all this mumbo-jumbo do you?" Matt asked Kofi.

"Many things have been revealed to me through the grace of almighty God. He came to me and instructed me thusly," said Kofi as he stood in the middle of the room, a strange aura surrounding his body while his breastplate shimmered with gold and sparkled with jewels, especially the Smithsonian's huge emerald.

"And thou shalt make the Breastplate of Judgment with cunning work. A span shall be the length thereof, and a span shall be the breath thereof. And thou shalt set in it settings of stones, even four rows of stones. The first row shall be a sardius, a topaz, and a carbuncle: this shall be the first row. And the second row shall be an emerald, a sapphire, and a diamond. And the third row a ligure, an agate, and an amethyst. And the fourth row a beryl, and an onyx, and a jasper," Kofi firmly and resonantly chanted with his arms outstretched, his eyes closed, and his body rhythmically swaying.

"They shall be set in gold in their enclosings. And the stones shall be with the names of the children of Israel, twelve, according to their names. Like the engravings of a signet, every one with his name shall they be according to the 12 tribes. And thou shalt make upon the breastplate chains at the ends of wreathen work of pure gold."

Matt tried to interrupt Kofi, whose trance-like speech and mannerisms were making all the officers uncomfortable. Kofi refused to be silenced as he stood in the middle of the room with arms outstretched, eyes firmly closed, his body vibrating to the sound of his voice, which methodically pounded out the instructions from God. They felt a strange wind come into the room and encircle Kofi's body which emanated an eerie glow that made the jewels on the Breastplate of Judgement radiate light in all directions. Two of the uniformed officers began backing toward the door of the room to give themselves running room as the atmosphere continued to intensify. Matt, who was standing closest to Kofi, looked at Jake who was mesmerized by Kofi's strident message.

"And thou shalt put the two wreathen chains of gold in the two rings which are on the ends of the breastplate. And they shall bind the breastplate by the rings thereof unto the rings of the ephod with a lace of blue that it may be above the girdle of the ephod that the breastplate not be loosed from the ephod."

Matt again tried to interrupt, but Kofi continued, his voice booming throughout the room, the third floor of the house, and the lower levels. The members of the Ife

Temple and their children who were gathered in the first floor meeting room hear his voice, dropped to their knees, and began to pray in unison.

"And thou shalt put in the Breastplate of Judgement the U'rim and the Thum'min; and they shall be upon Aaron's heart, when he goeth in before the Lord; and Aaron shall bear the judgement of the children of Israel upon his heart before the Lord continually."

Kofi dropped his head to his chest as he finished speaking. He continued standing in the middle of the room, his eyes closed, his arms outstretched, the breastplate of the High Priest gleaming on his chest. Matt walked over to him and touched his arm. Kofi slowly raised his head and looked at Matt.

"You're under arrest, Asante. Read him his rights, Jake."

Jake read Kofi his Miranda rights.

"That breastplate is evidence, Asante. Let's have it."

Kofi slowly and deliberately removed the breastplate, folded it in half, kissed it, and handed it to Matt.

"The word of the Lord has been spoken, Lieutenant Alexander. No man can interfere with the revealed word of God. The breastplate will be returned to me and I will be set free."

"Did you steal all of the stones in the breastplate?"

"The emerald was the only stone we took without paying for it."

"Yeah, right. Let that be a lesson to you, Asante. You should have thought about the consequences before you decided to break the law. Maybe Walter, Eddie, and Henry

Hughes would still be alive if you had."

"The emerald is the revealer of truth, and the enemy of magic and conjure. The person who possesses the emerald has the power to see the future, lieutenant. God has given me that power."

"Tell it to the judge, Asante," Matt said as he handcuffed Kofi again and led him back down the stairs. At the bottom of the stairs, a uniformed officer handed Matt the murder weapon, an exact duplicate of the six-foot long spear in the Stone Age Mammals exhibit.

"Good work, man! Where did you find it?" Matt asked the uniformed officer.

"In the basement. It was wedged into a crack in one of the ceiling beams."

Matt took the spear from the officer. In the meeting room, assembled members of the Ife Temple stood aside to let the officers through. The women and children sobbed as Kofi Asante was led through the temple in handcuffs.

"We've got your ass, Williams," Matt said to Carlos in the vestibule. "Read him his rights, Jake."

Kofi and Carlos were led out of the house to a squad car. Matt followed with the necklace, the Breastplate of Judgement, and the murder weapon. After they arrived at headquarters, Matt booked Kofi and Carlos. Then he went up to his office and placed a call to Lloyd Cullison.

"It certainly took you long enough to wrap this case up, Alexander."

"Thanks for the vote of confidence, Lloyd. What should I do with this $10 million necklace?"

"Jesus! What a pain in the ass? Can't you take it home

with you just for the night?"

"Not on your life, Lloyd. There's no way I'm taking the responsibility."

"Don't book it into property, Alexander. It's too big a risk."

"So where do we put it?"

"I'll call Kendricks and ask him to pick it up at headquarters. He ought to be glad to get it back since they didn't want it to leave the Smithsonian in the first place."

"Yeah, right," Matt replied to Lloyd before ringing off.

"Well, it looks like you made good on your promise to solve the Smithsonian homicide case this week, partner."

"Why don't I feel like celebrating, Jake?"

"It was a funky case. Everybody and his brother messing in it, trying to cover their own asses. We lucky we found the killers at all."

"It was a tough case" Matt replied as he alternately fingered the tumbled emerald necklace and the Breastplate of Judgement, which were lying on top of his desk.

"Man, this breastplate is something else," Jake said as he walked over to Matt's desk and touched the jewels on it. How much money you think they got tied up in this thing?"

"Who knows? I still can't figure Asante for believing all that mumbo-jumbo. Did you see how he was carrying on when he was wearing this thing?"

Jake quickly withdrew his hand from the breastplate.

"Yeah, I saw all that action. I think the dude is sanctified, Matt. He's blessed."

"Man, you need to get out of Dodge. Asante is a bona

fide fraud."

"Naw, partner. He's for real. I didn't want to believe it the first time I went to the temple, but after tonight I'm convinced he's a genuine prophet."

"He's a genuine thief. There's no question about that."

Wallace Kendricks arrived at Fourth District Headquarters at one-thirty in the morning. Willis Brandt and one other security guard were with him. Brandt and the guard waited outside in the corridor while Kendricks went into Matt's office and closed the door.

"I spoke to Secretary Marshall on the way over here, Alexander. He told me to thank you personally for recovering the emerald necklace."

"It's all in a day's work, Kendricks. There's no need to thank me," Matt handed Kendricks the cut necklace.

"What the hell happened to it?"

"Asante took one of the emeralds off so he could sew it on the Breastplate of Judgement," Matt replied as he showed Kendricks where the emerald was attached to the vest.

"It's a damn shame to ruin a priceless necklace for some tacky shit like that. Is that why they killed Hughes?"

"Kofi Asante didn't kill Henry Hughes. Carlos Williams killed him, and he didn't do it for the necklace."

"Didn't you recover the necklace from them?"

"Yes, I did, but Carlos Williams killed Hughes because Hughes killed Walter and Eddie Jones, the other two homicide victims. We found the murder weapon on Hughes' body, and he admitted killing them to both

Asante and Williams."

"Henry Hughes, since when?"

"Since he planted that fake on one of the two homicide victims he shot that Tuesday night in the museum." Matt insisted as Kendricks started to protest. "We all know that Henry Hughes had planned to steal the tumbled emerald necklace for at least a year. He had Herman Wittstein order the fakes for him; and he was just waiting for his chance. He got it the night Walter and Eddie Jones tried to use voodoo to steal the emerald necklace from the gem exhibit. He probably enticed them down to the African Village exhibit separately and shot them. The security system at the museum wasn't breached the night of the murders, because the necklace wasn't stolen until the next day."

"The next day. I don't believe you."

"You helped him steal it, Kendricks."

"That's a damned lie. I didn't know anything about the theft."

"That's true. You didn't know the necklace was being stolen from under your nose. But don't feel bad. All of us were standing in Hughes' laboratory when he made the switch."

"What the hell are you talking about, Alexander?"

"The genuine emerald necklace was never stolen, Kendricks. Hughes knew he had to plant one of the copies in such a way that you would think it was the original, because if you thought the genuine necklace had been stolen and a substitute put in its place, you would have to open the case to have the substitute examined by an expert, namely Henry Hughes. And, that's exactly what you did, Kendricks. Hughes lied when he said the necklace we found on the murder victim was genuine. It was one of his fakes. He didn't steal the genuine necklace until you and Brandt opened the case for him to examine it the day after the double homicide. When you opened the case on Wednesday, Hughes substituted the other fake Wittstein made for the genuine tumbled emerald necklace. It was a gem of a murder; and Henry Hughes outfoxed all of us."

"Looks like he outsmarted himself, ending up murdered like that. Where does Kofi Asante fit in Henry Hughes' murder?"

"I'm pretty sure he doesn't; but we'll nail him for stealing the necklace."

"We're not pressing charges on the theft," Kendricks asserted as he cut the lone emerald from the breastplate and placed it and the necklace in the velvet case he brought with him.

"Man, I don't believe this bullshit," Jake insisted.

"What the hell do you mean you're not pressing charges, Kendricks," Matt demanded.

"Just what I said. We've recovered the necklace, and if we don't press charges we don't have to report that it was stolen to our insurance company."

"What you mean is that you don't have to report the theft to the press and Capitol Hill."

"Have it your way, Alexander. Secretary Marshall has already discussed our decision with Commander Cullison, and he doesn't have any problem with it."

"If you don't report the theft, we don't have a case against Kofi Asante."

"Carlos Williams killed Henry Hughes; and you have a damned good case against him."

"Kofi Asante masterminded the whole thing. If it hadn't been for him, Walter and Eddie Jones would never have been in the museum the night they were killed in the first place. And if Henry Hughes hadn't killed them, Carlos Williams wouldn't have killed Hughes."

"I have my orders, Alexander. We're not pressing charges," Kendricks emphatically repeated as he got up to leave.

"You're all a bunch of self-serving hypocrites, Kendricks. Take your precious necklace and get the hell out of my office," Matt shouted as Kendricks hastily retreated.

"See what I told you, Matt. Kofi Asante said he wouldn't be charged and that he would get the breastplate back; and that's exactly what has happened."

"It's the Smithsonian's fault, Jake. They're still covering their asses."

"Maybe it's the Lord's doing, partner," Jake said as he left the office for the night.

After Jake left, Matt sat at his desk brooding over the case of the Smithsonian homicides. He fingered the Breastplate of the High Priest lying on the desk in front of him and thought back to Kofi's prediction that the vest would be returned to him and that he would go free. Matt silently cursed the police system he loved as he prepared to go home. He turned out the light and locked the door to his office, leaving the High Priest's breastplate on the top of his desk where it shimmered and gleamed in the dark emitting an eerie green light where the tumbled emerald had been cut.

THE END